Santorini

Inspired by a true story

By

Alex M Smith

This book was inspired by real people and real events but it remains a work of fiction. Some characters were combined to create different complex characters and most names, places and dates are fictional and any resemblance to actual persons, living or dead, organizations, events or locales are entirely coincidental.

Copyright © 2013 Alex M Smith

All rights reserved.

ISBN: 151972554X

ISBN-13: 978-1519725547

To Mom and Dad

CONTENTS

Kalispera	1
Who Would Ever Want to Leave this Place?	19
Meet Mr. Steele	31
Close Your Eyes and Jump	47
A Family Matter	61
Bed of Feathers	77
Beware of Greeks Bearing Gifts	93
We're Even	109
A Thousand Islands	121
Something Old, Something New, Something Borrowed, Something Blue	137
All I Know is that I Know Nothing	167

This book could not have been completed without the valuable contribution and dedication of my wonderful editor Tina

Kalispera

"Stay for the night," he pleaded as he pulled the sheets over his naked body.

"Spiro will be back in the morning," she said with a heavy English accent and seemingly unaffected by the intimacies they had just shared. "I have to catch the last ferry. It leaves the docks at six."

She adjusted her white cotton skirt that flowed softly nearly to her ankles; the light breezy fabric swirled around as she turned to admire herself in the mirror. She cocked her head to the side and lifted her hand up to one of her breasts, cradling it and lifting it slightly. She smiled when she saw Jack's reflection in the mirror, his sparkling blue eyes admiring her.

"You like, or I should make it bigger?" she asked, carefully studying her breasts. She let her blouse fall from her hand to the floor and pushed both of her breasts up further.

"They're perfect," Jack said with a smile and a wince of desire.

Dismissing his compliment, she let go of her breasts, quickly hooked her bra, and slipped her blouse on.

"You say that to all your women, Jack darling," she said as she closed the last button, leaving the upper two open, revealing her shallow cleavage.

"You make it sound as if I have hundreds of women lined up outside my door or stacked in my closet," Jack replied playfully but feeling slightly defensive. "Or I'm with a different woman every night."

He rose from the bed and crossed the room to stand beside her. Lifting her curly black hair from underneath the collar of her blouse, she glimpsed at his naked body and took out a pink lipstick from her purse. She applied it and smacked her lips together.

"Not every night. Every other night," she giggled as she fixed her mascara.

Jack left her side and put on his shorts and white linen pants. He stayed shirtless, showing off his well-toned upper body. He watched Aphroditi apply her makeup and change her look from a natural beauty to a magazine cover girl.

"I'm done," she announced, turning towards him. "How do I look?"

"Perfect," he said without looking.

She let out a long laugh.

"Men," she said and shook her head. "All you care about is this." She pointed to her body. "And never this," she added, putting her hand over her heart.

"Oh, boy," Jack said, anticipating a long lecture; he sat at the edge of the bed and stared at her.

"Would it have killed you to raise your eyes just a little bit to look at me?" she said, her voice louder but still playfully seductive.

Jack nodded and listened to her attentively; he tried to speak but was hushed by her second installment.

"You are like my husband," she said. "He comes back home after three months at sea, and he looks at me as if he saw a mermaid."

She lifted her skirt a little to show off her attractive legs then continued with more enthusiasm like an actress acting solo to a full theater.

"He hugs me and kisses me for three consecutive days," she declared, emphasizing her point by waving three fingers in the air. "He doesn't want to eat or drink or do anything else. All day and all night, he wants to be in bed with me."

Jack looked at a virtual watch on his wrist and looked back at Aphroditi.

"Jack, are you listening to me?" she asked, and without letting him answer, she continued. "Don't worry, I will not be late. You will get rid of me soon, but first, you have to listen."

Jack crossed his legs and looked at her and pretended to attentively listen.

"He reads me poetry and feeds me honey off his fingers, and if I want to get up, before my feet hit the ground, he carries me." She paused and held up three fingers again. "Three days, and that's it,"

She clapped her hands together, and Jack looked again at his virtual watch on his wrist then went back to Aphroditi, who was now calming down a little.

"After, he becomes tired, his reserves are all spent, he wakes up in the morning and goes out and comes back after midnight, sleeps like a log and rushes out the next morning without even saying *Kalimera*," she said with a dismissive voice.

She sat down on the chair next to the window facing the bed and continued.

"If I dare ask him where he went, my God!" she cried and raised both hands in the air. "As if I committed the ultimate sin." She suddenly looked at Jack with near contempt, not as someone she had just been intimate with. "You men are all like this."

"I'm not like that," Jack protested and approached her.

"Maybe not exactly," she said, quickly going back to her

spirited tone but her teasing words carried a sting. "But the moment that I go down the stairs and out of your sight, you will call your next woman." She laughed and held her hands out in front of her chest. "Bigger breasts woman." She then shouted loudly the most famous Greek curse, "*Malakas*".

Jack laughed at her very raw humor and her melodramatic scene as she quickly stood up and took his hand to check the time on her watch.

"*Appo*...I'm late. I have to run," she said, grabbing her shawl and handing it to Jack, who dutifully draped it over her shoulders. "If I can't catch the ferry, I have to stay for the night, and tomorrow, my Spiro will come here and cut off your..." she said playfully and paused for anticipation. "Your cute nose," she teased.

She stood on her tiptoes and gave him a peck on his nose then headed for the door. Jack smiled and shook his head. She turned and gave him a quick kiss on the lips.

"Don't forget to eat the pastries I brought you," she said, turning again to the door and opened it then quickly turned back to him. "And don't put the *baklava* in the fridge. It will become dry," she instructed.

"I'll eat it all now before my next woman arrives."

"*Moro mou*," she said and stopped him with her hand before he could escort her out. "I know the way. You stay here. I don't want your nosy neighbors to start talking," She gestured with her hand, opening and closing it to simulate the flapping jaws of gossiping mouths.

She stepped outside into the late afternoon sun and inhaled the sea air deeply

"Jack! Come quick!" she called.

He rushed to the door to see what the problem was.

"Can't you smell the air?" she asked and inhaled deeply again. She spread her arms and looked to the vast expanse of sapphire

Aegean Sea that spread before her as far as the eye could see. "It's the smell of a big storm coming."

Jack stepped out and slipped his arms around her waist and gave her a kiss on the back of her neck.

"You're adorable, you know that?"

"I know," she said playfully and freed herself from his grip. "A*ndio*," she called as she began to descend the steps, tracing her hand along the whitewashed wall that ran along the side of the stairway. The short wall was the only thing preventing someone from plummeting down onto another row of white and blue cubical homes below or into the shimmering sea below that.

Jack waited outside and watched Aphroditi's shadow disappear down the long stairs that wound down the steep hillside to the port below. She paused for a moment to pet a small stray kitten who walked on the wall, and when she passed by someone, and he heard her cheerfully say, "*Kalispera.*" He smiled at her compassion towards the cat and her friendliness toward a stranger and was warmed by the late afternoon sun but more so by the trail of bliss that she left behind her.

He watched until she was out of sight and was consumed again by the breathtaking view of the water. Although there were homes above and below him on the cliff, standing here overlooking the sea gave a feeling of solitude and standing on the edge of the world.

Physically she was out of sight, but her life-loving spirit would linger on until her next visit a few weeks later. He had been seeing her for more than two years now, and she hadn't changed a bit. Every time she came to the island, she brought with her joy and left taking away all the world's worries.

Even though it was late March and spring hadn't fully kicked in yet, the afternoon was relatively warm. The sea breeze was calmer than usual but strong enough to carry the refreshing scent from the white Madonna lilies, or *krinos* as they are known locally, that flourished around the main court and the entire island. There were no signs of an imminent storm in the cloudless sky above the serene island, but that could change in a matter of hours.

Aphroditi had wide, dreamy, soulful brown eyes and a round face with a petite nose and full cherubic lips. She was a couple inches over five feet tall, which made her stand on the tips of her delicate, well-manicured toes every time she reached to kiss Jack's lips atop his almost six foot tall posture. She had a narrow waist sitting on round sexy hips that led down to her sleek, toned legs. What set her apart, though, were her incredible outgoing spirit and her sarcastic sense of humor.

They met down near the port; he was there bidding goodbye to one of his friends who was visiting from Athens, and she was just arriving on her first visit to Santorini. He was drawn to her immediately, but before he could approach her, she came up to him and started speaking in Greek, thinking he was a local. His knowledge of the language at that time was limited to greetings and curse words. She laughed when she realized her mistake and used her limited English to ask for directions.

That night they met at a bar in town, and after a couple of drinks and her desperate attempts to teach him some dance moves, they went back to his place and stayed there until morning. Their relationship remained impetuous and passionate and was never misinterpreted between them. It stayed as simple as it began: two adults enjoying from time to time the company of each other.

Jack noticed the ferry coming through the caldera with its shadow reflecting on the crystalline sapphire sea around it and its engines leaving a white trail behind it. He had seen that sight a thousand times in the last three years. There are some things that would never change on the magical Greek island of Santorini: the glorious view of the brilliant blue water of the caldera, the lovely people, and the delicious food are eternal constants.

"Jack!" Nikos called cheerfully from downstairs. "Come down! Let's have some coffee and play *Tavli*." He stood in the courtyard carrying a backgammon board under his arm.

"*Tavli* is my favorite!" Jack shouted. "I'll take a quick shower and come down."

"You will catch a cold if you take a shower and go out," the distinct voice of Theodora called from behind Nikos. Her beautiful smile soon disappeared when she turned to Nikos and started arguing with him in Greek.

Jack overheard and translated a little bit of their conversation:

"You old man, keep walking fast so that you don't walk with me. Are you ashamed of me?" Theodora asked in an argumentative yet loving tone. "Men still give me the look you know," she continued as Jack went inside to take his shower.

To which Nikos replied, A scared look, "I'm sure, my love."

They were the sweetest, most charming old couple he had ever met.

Jack lived in Fira, the capital of Santorini, in a traditional Greek house on the east side of a cluster of houses that were turned into a small hotel. The seven houses each had the thick, whitewashed walls typical to the island of Santorini and still had the original 1960's furniture from when they were first offered for rent. Each house had a bedroom with one or two forged iron beds in it, a living room with a balcony, a bathroom, and a small kitchenette. The houses were adorned with blue shutters and trim and had brightly-colored flowers blossoming from terracotta pots near the entrance and in the courtyard. Privacy was insured by the thick volcanic stone walls, but the common areas in the central courtyard offered an inevitable intimacy between tenants. Only two houses sat on the upper level, and Jack had one of them.

Nikos was the caretaker, and he and his wife Theodora took

care of the tenants like they would take care of their own children. It was no wonder that vacationers who came here had a hard time leaving, as everybody adored the place and the sweet old couple who treated them with the traditional *filoxenia*, or hospitality, that was so typical of the Greeks. Jack was one of the guests who came in three years ago and was so enamored that he left behind his former life and stayed on the island.

He loved the serenity, the smells, and the tastes of Santorini. The contrasts also intrigued him: the wild parties that the tourists threw every summer night invigorated him, and the calm and peaceful traditional lifestyle that the locals provided during winter comforted him; the rugged, steep cliffs that the ancient volcano created thousands of years ago so unforgiving compared to the softness and tranquility of the people who lived above it. It was all of these things and more that pulled him in and inspired him to stay.

**

"You should marry this woman," Nikos said in between bites of his third piece of vegetable pastry that Aphroditi brought with her. "I married Theodora because of her good food." He paused for a second and added, "She was good in bed too."

Jack laughed as Theodora gave Nikos a smack on his arm as he was about to throw the dice. They flew from his hand, bouncing on the table then rolling down onto the floor next to the entrance.

"This is the wine speaking," Theodora said.

"You are drinking during Lent, old man?" Jack asked with eyebrows raised and a fake inquisitor's voice.

"God forgives nice people," Nikos replied.

"It's Annunciation Day, you fool," Theodora said and smacked Nikos on the back of the head. She looked at Jack and continued. "We celebrate because today Mother Mary knew she was pregnant with Christ."

Jack knew all the details of the Greek Orthodox faith; the last three years he spent on the island had taught him a lot. He learned how much faith wrapped with superstitions was part of the daily Greek life. Every step you take is accompanied by some higher power, be it from God or from an evil eye or from envy of a jealous neighbor. No matter what happens, you are never fully responsible for your actions.

Greeks during the Great Lent don't eat meat, poultry, or dairy products. Fish is allowed on very few occasions and wine on a few Saturdays as well as on Annunciation Day, which also happens to be the Greek National Day. Once Easter arrives, all of Greece becomes "*Meat Heaven*", and in front of every house, you see a skewered whole lamb roasting, and the entire country is filled with delicious aromas and the homes bursting with hospitality.

Jack was not Greek Orthodox, nor did he adhere to any religion for that matter, but he had to respect the local culture. He was a New Yorker by birth but a *Santorinian* by heart, as Theodora always told him. He never regretted for one day the big move he made from The City that Never Sleeps to the small island above a sleeping volcano. Ditching the business capital of the world to live in the center of one of the oldest cultures in the world was one big step towards peace of mind.

They sat under a vine-covered pergola in the middle of the courtyard. The buds started to break a week ago, and soon the courtyard would be filled with shade from the lush leaves, and by midsummer, it would be filled with dangling delicious red grapes. The place was magical in its simplicity and splendor, and it smelled like a bouquet of flowers. Today it was also adorned by small Greek flags since it was Independence Day. The small triangular flags blended in perfectly with the white homes with their blue rooftops, shutters and trim. On March 25, 1821, Bishop Germanos of Patras hoisted the Greek flag at the Monastery of Agias Lavras, sparking the Greek War of Independence.

Nearly two hundred years later on this day, there was a mini war of opinions between Nikos and Theodora. They were in their early sixties, a charming couple, who, like almost all Greek couples, constantly argued. It's a Greek habit to talk loudly and gesture while you're at it, adding dramatic elements to your words. They lived next door and were rarely away from home. They never left the island unless they needed to attend a wedding or a funeral of a relative who shamefully chose the mainland or the island of Crete as his or her home.

"Let's dance, my love," Nikos said to Theodora, holding her hand and trying to lift her off the chair as Jack walked towards the entrance to retrieve the rolling dice.

He could hear sounds coming from outside, the unmistakable clicks of donkey hooves climbing up the stairs. Donkeys were, in the past, the preferred way of transportation and the most effective way to navigate the labyrinth of steps that ran up and down the cliffs surrounding the famous caldera. Many places are accessible by car nowadays, and Fira is accessible by cable car from the ferry port below; however some still like to take the donkey ride up the six hundred steps. It is no easy ride for the donkey or the rider, but many tourists enjoy it and think it's the best way to travel despite its discomforts. The donkeys are laden with luggage and are ridden by the tourists while the owner walks besides them and guides them up the narrow, winding stairs to their destination.

As Jack walked back towards the lively old couple with Nikos still relentlessly trying to get his wife to dance with him, he heard a disruption in the rhythmic pattern of the donkey's hooves, a scuffle, and the sound of something falling onto the stone steps, followed by the distinct sound of a cry from a woman.

"*A damsel in distress*," Jack thought and ran outside. Nikos and

Theodora rushed out closely behind him, carried by the distinctive Greek helpful spirit and unleashed curiosity.

"Makis, you fool! Look what you have done!" Theodora scolded a scruffy middle-aged man who stood next to a grey donkey, trying to lift the woman who appeared unconscious.

"She's not moving," Nikos said as he crouched over her.

"Out of the way," Jack ordered as he lifted her off the ground and carried her through the blue wooden gate and into the courtyard. He reached the door and kicked it open then carefully laid the unconscious woman on a bed inside.

Nikos and Makis were still arguing outside when Theodora entered holding a bottle of rose water.

"Get the lights please," Jack said. "I'll call Doctor Vasilis."

As Jack used the front office phone to call the doctor, Theodora mixed some water with sugar and added a dash of rose water in it. Jack came in and confirmed that the doctor was going to be there in ten minutes. He checked the mystery woman and found out that she was breathing normally but was not responding to neither his calls nor to Theodora's gentle and light slaps on her face.

"She's a beauty," Jack exclaimed, noticing her for the first time. Her long brown hair mixed with golden locks lay softly across the pillow. He noticed her long eyelashes and soft kissable lips, then not to take advantage of her in her condition, he averted his eyes away from her exposed cleavage then noticed that her white dress was tainted by the fall and it was crumpled and lifted up to her hips, exposing most of her legs and thighs.

"This is all you can think off," Theodora snapped, noticing his wandering, lustful eyes, and lifted the cover off one side of the bed and draped it over the woman's body. "Go get her other sandal from outside," she ordered. As Jack was going out, she said, "Let that silly Makis get her things and put it in the room also and get me some wine too."

"You're gonna give her wine?"

"No, you silly boy, the wine is for me," she answered him, gesturing dismissively with her hand. "It keeps Nikos' and Makis' voices down," she continued muttering as Jack left.

Outside, a dozen people gathered around a very calm donkey. Voula and Dimitrios, the neighbors, and Yannis, their nine year old son, Maria and her fiancé Yiorgos, who is Nikos' and Theodora's son, and two of their friends who were visiting from the mainland all swarmed around the scene. They were all watching Nikos and Makis argue as the sun behind them was setting in magnificent shades of lavender, peach, and pink on the waters of the caldera and casting a lovely pastel tinge of color over the entire whitewashed village.

"You told me to make the donkey stop when it reaches your door!" Makis shouted.

"I told you to make it stop, not to kill somebody!" Nikos shouted back. "I want people to stay alive to maybe want to stay at my hotel."

"Oh! She's not dead, she's just sleeping," Makis explained, calming down a little. "Tired from the trip on the ferry," he added, rocking side to side to simulate a ferry rocking at sea.

"Yes, yes, Doctor Makis," Nikos said, mocking his diagnosis. "She's dead I'm telling you." He pointed an accusatory finger at him. "You're going to jail."

"She's not dead," Jack said, picking up her sandal.

"See?" Makis said to Nikos, pointing at Jack.

"You should go to jail anyways. You're too silly to be walking among people," Nikos said, helping Jack take the woman's luggage off the donkey.

"Why is this thing tied too tight?" Jack asked as he fought with the elaborately knotted rope, rocking the poor old donkey on its sturdy legs.

"Ask the idiot, who should have tied the woman tight,"

Nikos ranted again. "If the luggage falls, you buy a new one. The woman falls, it's the end."

"Papa, enough with this," Yiorgos said to his dad. "The woman is not dead. Jack told you. She's probably unconscious. All will be fine. Go help mama. I'll take care of this." He put his arm around Nikos and guided him away from the donkey then Jack stepped aside as Yiorgos untied the rope himself with relative ease.

"*Kalispera sas,*" a male voice called, breaking the tension between the men. A tall, thin middle-aged man wearing a suit and carrying a bag approached the group.

"Evening, Doctor," Jack said, reaching to shake the man's hand. Everyone else in the group greeted him as well.

"I got this," Yiorgos said, referring to the luggage and gestured to Jack to go in with the doctor.

***

"Does anyone know her name?" the doctor asked as he sat next to the unconscious woman. Nearly a dozen eager and concerned onlookers crowded the doorway and spilled into the room but gave the doctor and the mystery woman respectful space.

"Make way, please," Makis said as he came in with her luggage

"Is she dead, Doctor?" Nikos asked.

The doctor rolled his eyes in frustration and looked at Nikos shaking his head. He then took a small vial and passed it next to the woman's nose, and it immediately jerked her into consciousness.

"See, she's not dead," Makis said proudly.

"Ok, everybody out," the doctor ordered. "Except you, Dora."

As the doctor examined the woman, the party moved outside and the bickering continued. Nikos's face was turning red from anger again at Makis's carelessness, and he kept trying to see what was happening inside through the window despite that the curtains were closed.

"Her name is Katherina," Makis said finally.

"Now he tells us! Why not when the doctor asked?" Nikos snapped at him.

"I remembered it now," he said with a smile. "Very beautiful woman, very nice too. American. Paid me before she even climbed on the donkey." He patted his pocket which held the money.

"American, huh?" Jack said, "You can kiss that tip goodbye now."

"No, Mister Jack, she didn't kiss me only paid me," he said, not getting the joke.

"Yes, Makis, I understand. You can take your donkey and go home," Jack said, putting his hand on Makis's shoulder. "Isidora and the children must be waiting for you." He gently urged him towards the entrance and put a twenty Euro bill inside his pocket.

"Thank you, Mister Jack. You are always good to me," he said as he walked away with Jack following him to make sure that he left. "Isidora will make you nice mock *keftedes* and you come eat at our house."

"Of course I will," Jack said. "*Andio.*"

Jack dismissed everybody and was left with Nikos pacing back and forth, and he sat watching him and eating the last piece of pastry. Yiorgos offered to stay, but Jack insisted that he take his fiancée and friends and have fun for the night and assured him that he had everything under control, his father in particular, knowing that a crowd of well-wishers is still a crowd of too many opinions and he better do this alone.

"How are the preparations for Yiorgos's big day coming along?" Jack asked, trying to diffuse Nikos's anger.

"*Appo,* he forgot to tell you," Nikos said suddenly, stopping and putting his hand on his forehead. "Makis made him forget."

"What are you talking about?" Jack didn't understand what Makis had to do with Yiorgos's wedding.

"He wanted you to be his *breast* man," Nikos said, standing in front of Jack.

Jack laughed loudly. He got used to Nikos insisting on speaking English all the time with him, except that it was hardly English. The thing was that no matter how many times anyone tried to correct his hilariously incorrect sentences, Nikos insisted that what he spoke was the proper way of speaking. At first, Jack hardly understood anything or was able to keep himself from laughing, but three years later, he not only expected it, he loved it and he tried not to laugh as much.

"It would be an honor for me to be his *best man*," Jack said, tactfully correcting his word choice, and stood up. "I needed a reason to buy a new suit," he continued as he put one hand on Nikos's arm. "Will order it from Athens first thing tomorrow." He paused and looked Nikos in the eyes. "Now tell me. What's bothering you, old man?"

"Nothing," Nikos said and turned away, walking towards the window to take a peek inside. He then walked back towards Jack and started pacing back and forth again. Jack knew there was something more on his mind but didn't want to push him when he was already irritated. Nikos continued his troubled pacing and glancing at the house when he suddenly unleashed what was bothering him.

"How dare he call her Dora?" he asked angrily. "She's not his friend. She's not his sister. She's not his lover. *I only* call her Dora." He pounded his hand on his chest when he said the word "I".

Jealousy was the reason for all that anger then, Jack thought, still watching Nikos go back and forth and muttering incomprehensibly to himself. He then went up to his room and brought the sweets that Aphroditi made for him. Nikos eyes widened when he saw Jack putting it on the table and taking the lid off the plastic container.

"Mmmm... delicious," Jack said as he ate one piece and licked his fingers. "Nikos, Dora isn't even Greek. He calls her like this because he lived a long time in England, and it's common practice to shorten names. That's all that there is."

Nikos kept pacing back and forth and took a glimpse of Jack putting another piece in his mouth. His outrage was doubled now with the doctor doing God knows what with his wife inside and with the temptation that Jack was torturing him with outside. He stopped and took another peek at the window and looked at Jack who was biting on his third piece of delicious sweets.

"Nikos," Jack called, holding the plastic container up and offering it to him.

"It's a sin."

"It's a feast today," Jack answered, "Besides; the beautiful lady who made them, assured me that everything she used was vegetarian."

"No butter?"

"Absolutely not," Jack confirmed and took his fourth piece of baklava.

"Also vegetable cow?" Nikos said sarcastically.

"No cow milk, soy milk."

"I know you're lying," Nikos replied walking towards Jack and slowly picking one piece up with his fingers. The temptation was too great to resist.

"I am lying, but it is absolutely delicious," Jack said as he watched Nikos looking behind him, checking that his wife didn't see him eating. "Sit down, old man, and tell me what's bothering you,"

Jack patted the chair next to him, and Nikos reluctantly sat down and was quiet for a moment then finally spoke.

"I don't like Vasilis, that's it."

"It's all about that old story of him asking Theodora to marry him forty years ago?"

"I'm sure he's waiting for me to die to marry her," Nikos said after eating another piece of sweets.

Theodora, Nikos, and Vasilis were of almost the same age. They were neighbors as children, went to the same school together, and became inseparable. Vasilis's parents were well-to-do and owned many houses and land on the island, including the small hotel that Nikos runs today. They were very influential and well respected in their community, while Nikos came from much more humble means.

Nikos was in love with Theodora as far back as he could remember, but Theodora had her eye on Vasilis. His family was wealthier than Nikos's, he was more handsome, and all of the girls flocked to him. On her sixteenth birthday, Theodora let him kiss her; above all other girls, he had chosen her. Once his parents knew about their love, they sent him to a private school in Athens and later to medical school in London.

During this time, Theodora's parents urged her to get married, and at nineteen, Nikos and Theodora became husband and wife. Nikos was a strong, hardworking, and dependable man who was gentle and softhearted as well. Theodora knew that Nikos would provide security for her and he would make a great father for their children. In the meantime, Vasilis's parents decided to renovate the cluster of houses and turn them into a small hotel. Nikos and Theodora became their caretakers at that point, and Nikos essentially worked under the man who he still harbored resentment towards.

To the disappointment of Nikos, Theodora never got pregnant, even after ten years of marriage. No kind of treatment seemed to work, traditional or medical. They visited fertility specialists and tried homeopathic remedies, but Theodora remained barren until Vasilis came back from England. He brought with him a new wife and baby daughter. Two months later, Theodora was pregnant amidst rumors of foul play.

Nikos, who was supposed to be happy that he was soon going to be a dad, was instead devastated by the rumors of his beloved wife being with another man. The rumors were shattered, however, once Yiorgos was born and he had a birth mark on his left arm in the exact place and shape as the one on his dad's arm. His father, of course, was unmistakably Nikos after all.

Despite all that, Nikos's insecurities towards Vasilis never ended, and he took great measures to maintain distance between them. He remained very loving and protective of Theodora, which, aside from being a devoted husband, also served to shelter her and keep a greater distance between her and Vasilis.

Although Vasilis was technically Nikos's employer, he never had a single conversation about the business with him. Every month, Nikos took out his salary and sent the rest to Vasilis's father. Once his father died, he sent it to his mother, and once she died, he sent it directly to Vasilis but never once dealt directly with him and avoided contact with him as much as possible. Vasilis being the local doctor, however, ensured he would continue to have necessary contact with Theodora and her family, much to Nikos's chagrin.

Who Would Ever Want to Leave this Place?

The light was off in the room when Katherine woke up, but from the glow that the heavy crimson drapes emitted, she could tell that it must be almost noon. She sat up in bed, rubbing her eyes and trying to recall the events of last evening. Although she remembered almost everything that happened after she woke up, the events leading up to her being in the cozy hotel with strangers around her were still all blurry in her mind.

The room still smelled of the rosewater that Theodora brought for her to drink. Doctor Vasilis didn't allow her to administer it in fear of giving her irregular heartbeats, but he let Theodora rub it on her face and arms. Katherine took a deep breath and smiled. She enjoyed the delicate scent of roses, and it had made her skin soft and silky. It made her feel pretty and feminine yet she still needed a bath and thought it might help clear her mind.

She rocked herself on the lush mattress several times to see if she got dizzy or her head hurt. Deeming it safe enough, she slowly got out of bed. She looked around for the light switch and found it next to the door. Walking in front of the window covered with red light and the warm midday sun, she reached the light switch and switched it on.

She squinted in the sudden change of light, and, for a few seconds, she was totally blind. She gradually opened her eyes and looked around. The room was smaller than she originally thought, and the white walls looked thick and the windows small. The décor had a modest, wholesome appeal, and the furniture was antique yet very well maintained and beautiful. Even the door, which was a little bit over six feet high, had an arched top and forged iron handles. It seemed for a moment she had traveled back in time, far from the modern, high-tech world to which she had grown accustomed to after spending six weeks in Japan.

Her suitcase and handbag were neatly placed next to the small oak wardrobe. She walked towards it, opened it, and found the dress she was wearing yesterday neatly hanging in the closet. She examined it, and to her surprise, it didn't have any evidence of a fall. The dirty patches and the wrinkles had vanished; even the rip under the arm was gone. Some fairy must have taken it fixed it and returned it while she slept.

She opened the second wardrobe door and found what she was looking for. On the inside of the door was a full length mirror, the friend and foe of every living woman. She looked at herself, and when she saw her pink nightgown reflection in it, she remembered exactly what happened.

She got off the ferry and looked around and found a man with a donkey waiting. She was already dizzy from the seven-hour ferry ride and before it the long twelve-hour flight. At that time, she regretted not staying the night in Athens to recuperate before traveling on to Santorini. She also regretted choosing the ferry instead of the airplane.

At the time, the idea of traveling to an island by sea sounded nice, but soon after the ferry started moving through the waves, the romance of sea travel was replaced with discomfort to say the least. She tried to take a nap on the ferry, but the sounds and constant rocking kept her awake. She also regretted taking a donkey ride, no matter how quaint and charming that idea sounded at the time. She could have easily taken a taxi and none of this would have happened.

Katherine, Makis, and the poor donkey started climbing up the stairs leading to the top of the thousand-foot cliff. The climb was slow, and she kept thinking of how hard was it on the donkey to have to carry her and her luggage. She wanted to get down and walk, but she was too tired to even climb down off of the donkey, not to mention carry herself up the never-ending, winding stairs.

Makis kept talking; she tried to concentrate on what he was saying. It was all about the history of Santorini and the volcano eruption that took place thousands of years ago, bringing the Minoan presence on the island to an abrupt and tragic end. The dizzying height as they ascended the steps, the motion of the donkey's gait, and Makis's non-stop history lesson became overwhelming, and at that point, the donkey stopped, and everything for her blacked out.

She woke up to the sight of a smiling old woman and a man ordering everyone to get out of the room. It took her a couple of minutes to realize where she was. The doctor told her that she was suffering from mild dehydration and exhaustion, nothing that a long sleep and six cups of water with electrolytes wouldn't cure.

He was obviously Greek, judging from his looks, but his accent was distinctly British. She heard a few voices outside her room, but they soon subsided. The doctor left a few minutes later, making sure that she drank her first glass of homemade electrolyte drink, which the nice old lady prepared for her and insisted on helping her drink while she helped her hold the glass. She was ready to sleep, but again the woman insisted that she change into her nightgown and even helped her out of her dress and into it then guided her back to lay her head on the pillow again. She then laid the soft blanket over her and tucked her in as if she were a child.

Looking at the dress, she knew the reason behind all that

insistence. She remembered that the lady carried her dress with her once she turned off the lights and left. This woman had, in fact, cleaned and repaired her soiled and torn dress. This wasn't, after all, a Cinderella story with singing mice that could sew or the work of fairies, but it was the best personalized service she had ever gotten from a hotel in her life. She felt calm and relaxed as if she were at home. This was even better than home, though, since at home, she didn't have anyone to give her such amazing tender, loving care.

Before she closed the wardrobe, she got a hairbrush out of her handbag and brushed her hair. She then went and poured herself a glass of water from the clear water jug and drank the full glass without stopping. Katharine looked for the bathroom door, but she couldn't find it. There was only one door in the room, and she was sure that it would lead to the courtyard that she saw when she peeked out from the closed drapes.

Damn.

She whispered under her breath at the notion that she had to share a bathroom with someone else. Every small apartment, on the contrary, had its own bathroom, except that it was not ensuite. In the old days, it wasn't considered healthy to have the bathroom door connected to the house. Everything had to be kept separate: you slept in one place, you ate in the other, and you did your business and bathed somewhere else.

Remembering that she had read this in a travel guide book, that meant that she would have to venture outside of her room to locate the facilities. She put on her slippers that were neatly stowed under the bed and reluctantly walked towards the door. She wished that she could hold herself a little bit longer, just until she checked out and got to her original hotel, a modern hotel with services accessible from inside the room. To wait that long wouldn't be humanly possible, so she gathered a bit of courage and started her journey.

She opened the door, and a gust of fresh air and warm sunlight gently hit her face. Then another breeze followed, this time carrying the scent of jasmine mixed with a dozen other delightful scents. *Heavenly*, she thought as she closed her eyes and took a deep breath, letting the aromas fill her lungs and her spirit. When she opened her eyes, she almost forgot what she wanted so urgently to do when she woke up.

The scene in front of her was certainly taken out of a painting the artist dreamed about. *It can't be real*, she thought and blinked her eyes several times to make sure that she wasn't imagining things. *It must be the fall that caused all this,* a voice in her head told her. She even lifted her hand and tried to touch the beautiful painting in front of her.

The cluster of bright white houses was over two levels surrounding the court from three sides. The fourth side was open to the caldera below and the azure sea that filled it. The brilliant colors of the sky and the sea blended together at the horizon, and Katherine couldn't distinguish where the sea ended and the sky began. It seemed to be an otherworldly mirage in its stunning beauty.

She took her first step then the second then the third over the old stone floor and kept walking until she reached the edge overlooking the caldera. The wind grew stronger as soon as she was outside the shelter of the house walls. Her hair blew and her nightgown fluttered in the strong breeze, and her lungs filled with the fresh clean scent of the sea and the plentiful flowers that blossomed around her.

To her left, she could see the winding stairs in between clustered white houses and small churches with cobalt blue-domed roofs and bell towers with their multiple tiny bells. In the vast caldera below, she could see a ferry leaving the port, just like the one she came in on yesterday, and she wondered, *Who would ever want to leave this place?*

To her right was a similar breathtaking view of radiant white homes and everywhere a resplendent vista of the sea. The panoramic view looked like postcard of an exotic locale that one would dream of one day traveling to but never actually have a chance of visiting, but more than that, she thought, she truly must have died and found herself now in a paradise.

She hesitantly turned around and walked back towards her room, not wanting to take her eyes off of the dazzling sight in front of her and hoping that her hotel would be as nice and serene as this one. As she walked away from the caldera view, she looked up at the houses above hers, forgetting for a moment that she had gone out to find the bathroom. She could see the shadow of a man looking out of a window. The man smiled when he saw her looking at him, and she shyly smiled back and looked away.

Jack was in his room sitting at his writing table. He was typing the last sentence of Chapter Nine in the book he was writing. He had just looked up and saw the woman who he had rescued the night before walking through the court. She looked beautiful in the sunlight, nearly angelic with her flowing golden locks and gauzy nightgown set adrift in the breeze. Her face glowed when she smiled back at him.

He leaned back in his chair once she disappeared from his line of view. He had been up writing since six and certainly needed a break. He rubbed his eyes and took the paper out of the 1950's Smith Corona Sterling Super-5 manual typewriter. He placed it face down on top of a growing heap of papers, placed a paperweight on top of it, and opened his window. He took a deep breath and walked out to the kitchen and made himself a feta cheese sandwich with cucumbers, tomatoes, and a few black olives. A few minutes later, he prepared himself a cup of Greek coffee and carried the small cup and kettle down to the courtyard.

Katherine, in the meanwhile, had located the bathroom and

had a quick bath, although disappointed to wash the fresh smell of roses off her skin. She went back to her room and put on a dress and packed her things. Once she was ready, she headed out of her room. This time instead of the smell of jasmine, she was greeted with the smell of fresh coffee in the courtyard.

"Kalimera," Jack said, turning back to greet her.

"Kalimera," she answered slowly, not sure if she pronounced it right.

"It means good morning, in case you were wondering," he said, standing up and turning around as she walked towards him.

"I know what it means," she said, holding up a miniature phrase book.

"I see you came prepared," he said with a smile. "I hope you are feeling better today."

"Much better, thank you. I'm as good as new."

"You were very light though, but don't do that again."

Katherine was a little perplexed by what Jack just said and wondered if she got exactly what he meant.

"You're the one who carried me?"

She paused for a second as he smiled, trying to remember being in the arms of such a handsome man.

"But I only saw an older man and woman."

"Doctor Vasilis and Theodora."

"Right."

"You scared a lot of people yesterday," he said then realized that it was totally overdramatic. He didn't want to worry her, so he added, "Including an old donkey."

Katherine laughed when she started to imagine what it would have looked like from someone else's point of view as she clumsily slipped in a lifeless lump off of the donkey who was packed full of luggage.

"I'm Jack, by the way," he said waiting for her to respond.

"Katherine," she said, after pausing for a second. "I remember hearing the name *Zack* and thinking that this couldn't be possibly a Greek name."

"It would be if it was Zeus," Jack joked. "They were probably saying my name, but since the Greeks don't have the letter J, they turn it in to a Z sound."

"You're American, right? I mean from the accent and all."

"So are you."

"Here it's safe to say I am. In some countries, I had to pretend and say I'm Canadian to avoid hostile looks."

"Especially with all the wars we are waging nowadays. So you've visited many countries?" he asked then remembered his manners. "Sorry I didn't offer you any coffee. Would you like to have some?"

"Oh, no thank you. I probably ought to get going. Oh, and Greece will be my thirty eighth."

"Impressive," he said and noticed that she started looking around for something, "The reception is through that door." He pointed her in the direction of another blue door with bougainvillea blooming above it; to her it looked like every other door that she had seen. "And the guy's name is Nikos. If he's not there, he's probably taking a nap in the next room. Just call his name, and he will come out."

"Thank you. I'm really sorry, but I have to go. It was nice meeting you and sorry if I caused you any trouble yesterday," she said and started walking away.

"Nice meeting you too, Katherine," he said, sorry to see her leave so quickly. "Come visit sometime. You don't have to fall down. Just walk in."

She laughed as she walked towards the reception door, and Jack took a long look at her as she walked away. She had a raw natural beauty, and he thought she looked right in place on the island.

He kept watching as she opened the door; she looked back at him, smiled, and went in.

***

Nikos was indeed taking a nap when Katherine entered the empty reception area. He was sitting in his chair behind his desk with a newspaper in his lap and his eyes closed. He was snoring peacefully, and Katherine thought this must be the relaxing effect that the island had on everyone. He woke up as soon as he heard the door close, and the newspaper fell to the floor as he stood up. His smile was more of seeing a long lost friend or a son or daughter coming in for the holidays after a year away than just greeting a customer of the hotel.

Katherine heard the sound of a sewing machine when she came in. The sound stopped for a moment and then continued, but once she started to talk, the sound stopped again, and an old woman who Katherine recognized as Theodora came in to greet her.

She remembered the smile on her face from yesterday. The old lady came near and gave Katherine one kiss on each cheek. Katherine blushed and didn't know what to say or how to respond. She just stood there and smiled.

"Nikos, don't just stand there! Get the girl a chair," Theodora ordered in Greek, and Nikos complied.

Katherine was about to protest and say she had to be on her way but couldn't continue once she was led into Nikos's chair while he brought another one from the next room.

"You must be hungry, my dear," Theodora said. "I will get you something to eat."

Katherine opened her mouth to turn down the offer when Theodora continued.

"Did you drink the juice I made you?"

Katherine nodded.

"It was very delicious, thank you," she said graciously. "But I really have to go now."

"Eat and then go," Theodora said and left the room, winning the argument.

"Mr. Nikos, I have a reservation in another hotel, and I need to go there," Katherine said as Nikos sat himself on the chair that he had just carried in. "I want to know how much I owe you."

"Owe me?" Nikos said with surprise. "For what?"

"For last night, for the room," she explained. "And also for fixing my dress."

"Oh, nothing. You don't owe me anything."

"I don't understand."

Theodora suddenly barged in carrying two dishes in her hands.

"This we call *Fava Pantremeni Tis Santorinis*," she announced proudly. "It's yellow split peas, and this is *Pseftokeftedes Santorinis*, tomato fritters."

"They look delicious," Katherine said. "But I really have to get going, and I never thanked you for fixing my dress."

"No need to thank me, "Theodora said humbly. "Come. Let me show you."

She took Katherine's hand and pulled her off the chair, and before she could object, she was standing in the next room, which was filled with bolts of fabric, lace, and the table was strewn with lace trim, thread, and every accoutrement needed by a seamstress. Katherine was astonished when she saw the wedding dress that hung on a dressmaker's form next to the sewing machine.

"This is so beautiful," she said with amazement.

"Pure silk," Theodora said and put Katherine's hand on it.

"It's so soft...and this beadwork is exquisite. For your daughter?" Katherine asked as she continued touching the dress like it was a museum piece.

"For my son," Theodora said proudly, and when she saw the surprise on Katherine's face, she laughed and corrected herself. "My son's bride. They will get married in three weeks."

"I'm sure she will look adorable in the dress."

"You should come to the wedding. I'll make you a dress," Theodora suggested without giving Katherine a choice in the matter and almost immediately started taking her measurements.

Katherine was too shy to object, and by now, she learned that no matter what she said, she would not win, so she went with it. It took Theodora a couple of minutes to take the measurements. She wrote them in a notebook that had hundreds of other measures and made a short note in Greek under what Katherine assumed was her name.

"I really have to go," Katherine said with urgency.

"You want Nikos to help you with your luggage? Jack is here. He can help you too," Theodora said as they walked back to the reception. "Jack is a very nice man. He writes books."

Katherine was flattered by all of this attention and hospitality, and before she could reply, Theodora added, "Not married also."

"I want to know how much I owe you for the night and for fixing my dress, and I want the address of the doctor to pay him too." Katherine said, ignoring Theodora's comments about Jack.

"Doctor Vasilis will tell you first fall for free, second fall, you pay," Theodora said jokingly. "And you don't owe us anything."

"But I stayed for the night, and you fixed my dress."

"Nikos, tell her why we don't want her money."

"You didn't come to sleep here. You were going up to your hotel and you fell. If Theodora falls in front of your house, God forbid, and you take her in, you charge her for the night?"

"Of course not," Katherine replied, touched by their generosity. "But that's different."

"It's the same for me," Nikos said, ending the argument.

"Eat something before you go," Theodora urged her again.

Katherine's cell phone rang before she could answer.

"I'm sorry. I have to take this. First call on my Greek number" Katherine said and excused herself to take the call.

This is she speaking.

The reason that I was a no show was that I had a medical emergency.

I will be there in less than half an hour.

I don't understand why you have to charge me for last night.

Ok, I understand, but that's not fair.

It's the low season, I'm sure you had plenty of empty rooms other than mine.

One minute please.

Katherine covered her phone and turned to Nikos.

"Is the room still available?"

"Of course it is, and if it wasn't, we will put you in our house."

Katherine looked at Nikos and Theodora and smiled and went back to her phone call.

Please cancel my reservation.

Yes, I understand that you have to charge for last night and for tonight.

"I'll take the room," Katherine said after ending her call and handed Nikos her credit card.

"You give me this when you decide to leave," Nikos said and gave Katherine her card back.

"Now eat something," Theodora said.

Meet Mr. Steele

It's extremely rare in cities or communities to find practically all directions you give and get are either "up the hill" or "down the hill" instead of "take a right turn", "go east", or simply "straight ahead". In most parts of Santorini, everything is located either "above" or "below" another location on the rugged slope of the island. Ups and downs become your life, not only metaphorically but also physically.

Jack was climbing the stairs for the tenth time that afternoon. He was helping a friend of a friend move some furniture from his house to his daughter's house almost fifty steps uphill. While the maze of stone steps between the homes made a unique and striking sight on the island, carrying furniture up those stairs was not the easiest task.

It was just after five, and Santorini was coming back to life after a long-deserved afternoon siesta. The lagoon below had changed to a deep indigo at the shoreline as the sun began to set. As the sun dipped below the horizon, the silvery-blue waters would become mysterious, deep shades of amethyst and plum.

"Awww," Jack cried in pain as he bumped in someone rushing to get out of the hotel main entrance.

"I'm so sorry," Katherine said. "Are you Ok?"

"You know, we should stop meeting like this"

"I wasn't looking… I didn't mean to… I think you need to put some ice on that."

"I'm fine. Don't worry," Jack said, examining his nose.

It wasn't bleeding, and it wasn't broken, but it took a strong bump from Katherine's head. A couple of tears ran down his cheeks, normal when you get a hit on the nose. Jack wiped them out as quickly as he could in case the beautiful woman thought he was crying. He was also amazed that she didn't feel a thing. *That woman was surely hard-headed to take all those bumps on her head and survive unscathed*, he thought.

"I was running away," Katherine said, explaining her rush. "Looking behind me to see if someone was following me to make me eat, again."

Jack laughed despite the pain his nose was causing.

"You sure should put ice on this," Katherine said, taking a closer look at Jack's nose. It was red and beginning to swell.

"I will ask Nikos for some ice."

"I have ice in my room," Katherine offered. "I don't think it will be a good idea to wake Nikos up." She lowered her voice and leaned in toward Jack and added, "He might want to offer you food to cure you."

Jack laughed again at Katherine's take on her food experience just after spending less than one day on Greek soil.

"Don't worry; dinner won't be served before ten. Greeks eat very late," Jack said as he and Katherine walked towards her room.

***

Alexandrino was a small bar built in one of the caves on the caldera. Its cozy, warm atmosphere with low lighting was accompanied by traditional Greek music coming from old vinyl records. Half a dozen patrons could sit along a narrow bar and a dozen more around the tables surrounded with wall seats. It would open its doors around sunset every evening and would close when the last patron calls it a night.

Yiorgos was the sole owner and employee of the place. During summer when tourists flocked in droves to the island, he would hire some temporary help and usually a friend would pitch in and do the work for a glass of cold beer. It had always been that way at Alexandrino, and Yiorgos intended to keep it that way.

A few of his regulars were already installed in their usual places at the bar. Two of them even helped him open and lowered the bar stools. Four were locals, and two were a retired English couple, long-term residents of Santorini.

"That was absolutely amazing," Katherine said, entering the bar with Jack who was greeted by everyone who turned as soon as they walked in.

"*Yia sas!*" he called to everyone as Katherine showed them a huge smile.

"Lizzy, beautiful as ever," Jack said, taking the hand of the English lady and bringing it up to his lips. "Bertie," he added, greeting her husband.

"Haven't seen you for a long time, old chap," Bertie said. "What brings you here?"

"I was showing Katherine the famous sunset from in front of Alexandrino," Jack said, "Katherine, this is Elizabeth and Albert Kelly from Liverpool, and this is Katherine from…"

"San Francisco," Katherine said.

After the introductions, Lizzy and Bertie invited Katherine and Jack to join them. The couple was in their late sixties, both retired public servants. Lizzy worked in the Cabinet Office and Bertie in Her Majesty's Treasury.

"So you're the girl who fell off the donkey," Lizzy said.

"Oh my God, you know about that too?" Katherine asked with surprise.

"We live on a small island, my dear. If you don't want anyone to know about something you've done, you better not do it."

"That would be my last fall."

"What would you like to drink?" Jack asked Katherine.

"Any local specialties?"

"Best wine in Greece, courtesy of volcanic ash," Bertie suggested.

"And that's why you're drinking beer," Katherine commented with a smile.

"I'm English. I can't help it."

"I'll take the wine, thank you," Katherine said to Jack.

"Another round?" he said asking the Kellys.

"That would be splendid," Bertie answered.

They spent a few minutes talking about Katherine's fall before the conversation turned to Santorini, and Katherine couldn't stop talking about how beautiful the sunset was over the caldera. They also talked about how nice it is to have such hospitality and generosity among the locals but it also comes at the price of having limited privacy.

"Here you are, Bertie, Lizzy, Jack, and Katherina," Yiorgos said as he placed the pints of beer and the two glasses of local white wine.

Katherine didn't know how the bartender knew her name and kept looking at him until he noticed.

"I'm Yiorgos, Nikos and Theodora's son; I was an eye witness to the fall last night."

"And I was wondering how you knew my name. Your dad and mom are adorable."

"Would you like to order any food? It's homemade by no other than my adorable mother."

Katherine lifted her hand in protest. "Oh, no, no..." she said. "Thank you. Your mother fed me enough today."

"*Stin yia mas*," Yiorgos said before leaving the table, and everyone but Katherine said the same.

"That was 'Cheers' in Greek," Jack said to Katherine.

"I kinda figured it out, but couldn't say it on time."

"You can just say *Yiamas* like I do," Lizzy suggested. "Shorter form and same meaning."

Lizzy and Bertie first visited Santorini eleven years ago, and they fell in love with the island and its warmth and scenic views. Once they retired, they bought a small house, and they called it home for the past seven years. They only go back to England during the summer, avoiding the tourists season and to have the chance to spend some time with their daughter and three grandchildren. With the 2004 Summer Olympics taking place in Athens this year, coming back to its roots, the situation all over Greece would be even more hectic.

It felt a little bit weird for them at first, but they learned how to adjust to the culture. In their home country, you are formal with members of your own family, and they take an appointment to visit your home. Here in Santorini, you ask for directions, and they invite you for a cup of coffee at their house, followed by dinner that lasts until midnight.

What was difficult was to adjust to the loose form in which people used the word "tomorrow". The word doesn't mean exactly the day following today. It usually means some time in the future. It also makes everything circumstantial and unpredictable, but somehow everything works and things eventually get done, and get done well for that matter, without the pressure of deadlines.

"Another round?" Jack asked.

"Not for us," Bertie said, finishing his pint.

"We are meeting someone for dinner," Lizzy clarified as she

stood up. "Was nice meeting you, Katherine, and Jack, please bring her along and let's do something together sometime."

"I would love that," Katherine said.

"Don't stay late. It looks like there will be some rain later tonight," Lizzy warned.

"It's already taken care of," Jack said to Bertie as he asked Yiorgos for the bill.

"Next time will be on us then," Bertie said. "Have a nice time, you two, and nice meeting you, Katherine. Stay off donkeys for a while." Katherine cringed inside to be reminded again of her embarrassing moment but only smiled politely. He then pointed to Jack and said, "Or you will end up with him carrying you to bed."

***

The walk to Alexandrino had taken an hour, although it was only five minutes away from Katherine's hotel. After icing his nose for ten minutes, Jack decided to take her on a tour along the caldera. He started telling her the history of the island and the Minoan civilization that thrived there, how it was cut short by one of the largest volcanic eruptions of all times. Listening to Jack's voice telling the story was soothing and melodic to her ears, much unlike the last time she heard the story while she was rocking and woozy on donkey-back; she hung on his every word as if he were a great storyteller of ancient times. She commented that all good things end with a tragedy and also all good things start with a tragedy, since this beautiful crescent island was crafted by the same volcanic eruption that destroyed its glorious past.

Katherine was mesmerized not only by Jack's storytelling but also by the lagoon formed by the collapsed volcano. The sun blazed orange, about to be extinguished by the sea that shimmered and glowed in gradient shades of cerulean blue like her eyes and gold like the sun-kissed strands of her hair. The shades of gleaming copper nearest the sun later gave way until the entire caldera was filled with rich jewel-like purples and plums. The only words she could find in the vast English vocabulary were: *It's absolutely amazing.*

Jack was smitten by Katherine's interest in the island and the way she absorbed every word that he spoke. She anticipated each word like she craved it, and it gave him a great feeling of importance and satisfaction to feel her focus on him. Truthfully, the hypnotic quality of his voice had such an impact on her that he could have been talking about his grandmother's phlebitis and she would have found it fascinating. Jack, on the other hand, had a hard time keeping track of where he was in the story and had to concentrate because he was distracted by Katherine's beauty as the setting sun illuminated her ivory skin and set her silken hair aglow with gilded streaks of light.

The wind had slightly picked up and lifted her hair from her shoulders in the breeze, a sight that hit Jack in the center of his being as it revealed the delicate, tender skin of her elegant neck. The storm that Aphroditi had predicted was approaching quickly from the north. From his experience on the island, he estimated that it was still six hours away, but it would be a welcome sight. Rainy days on Santorini were rare, even during winter, but when they came, it brought desperately needed water to replenish the island's wells.

Jack promised to take her on a more elaborate tour of the island during her stay. She loved his knowledge of history, and she loved more the way he presented it. He was a wonderful story teller, and everything came to life as the words came out of his mouth. She could easily see a whole civilization with its people, cities, arts, culture, and everyday life in his words.

***

"Theodora told me that you are a writer," Katherine said once Jack came back to the table after bringing their third round of wine himself.

"She was telling the truth," Jack said with a smile.

"I'm sure she was, and she happened to mention that you are not married."

"She probably said that to half of the girls on Santorini and all the women who stayed at the hotel."

"And no one took the bait for the most eligible bachelor on an island!" Katherine started laughing before she finished her sentence.

Jack just smiled and took a sip from his chilled glass of wine.

"So any books that I might have read?" Katherine enquired with a more serious tone.

"If you like female sleuth stories."

"I read a few."

"Perry Street, Wakeup Call, Upstate, Hookup…" Jack recited the names of four books.

"I read Perry Street. I also saw the movie." She paused for a second then added "But I don't remember the author's name."

"R. J. Steele," Jack said, correcting her and grinning.

"Exactly."

"I liked the book more than the movie, by the way."

"They made too many changes that I would never have approved of, but unfortunately I didn't have a say in it."

"How come? It's your book?"

"Once you transfer the movie rights to the studios, they can practically do whatever they want."

"That's bad."

"Unless you're the J.K. Rowling of the world, you're completely out of control," Jack stated. "But I was happy to get the hefty check."

"I'm sure. So R. J. Steele is your real name or a pen name?"

"Funny story; have you ever seen the television series *Remington Steele*?"

"With Pierce Brosnan and Stephanie Zimbalist."

"That's the one."

"I loved it."

"Me too. I used to watch it all the time, although I was only twelve when it started, but something about it captured me and made me want to write."

"So you chose R. Steele as homage to Remington Steele," Katherine deduced. "I totally get it and you kept J. for yourself."

"You took the words out of my mouth."

"And that man was so damn handsome," Katherine said with dreamy eyes.

"Thank you."

"Wipe that smile off your face; I was talking about the real Steele."

"Need another?" Jack asked, pointing to Katherine's almost empty glass.

"Are you trying to get me drunk, Mr. Steele?"

Jack started typing on a virtual keyboard.

"He offers her another glass of wine, her fourth for the night, hoping to get her guard down. She resists at first, dreading the obvious…"

"Then she looks deep in his eyes and leans forward," Katherine continued, acting out her words. "Her lips brushing against his ear, her warm breath making him flush with anticipation…"

Jack, in fact, became all red as Katherine came close to him and her scent mixed with her wine-laced breath engulfed him. She could feel the warmth of his breath against her skin as she leaned into him.

"She opens her lustful lips and whispers in his ear," Katherine continued softly then paused, building Jack's anticipation as she put her left hand over his shoulder. "Which door leads to… the ladies room?"

***

Greeks don't eat alone for a reason. The social nature of the people makes them want to always get together around a table, and the nature of their food makes it easy to turn a meal into a social event. Greek food mostly consists of small dishes shared by everybody sitting at the table. If more people show up, more food is ordered; if the people need more variety, they order different dishes. It is common to see a table almost completely covered with twenty different dishes, shared by only three or four people.

Also what's remarkable is that when you enter a Parisian restaurant, for example, it is so quiet that the only thing you hear is the sound of forks and knives. In contrast, your entrance into a Greek restaurant is greeted by lively, colorful conversation and laughter mixed all together. Greeks also know their food and know where to eat. If you are a tourist and you see a place with only tourists in it, do not enter, and only eat where locals do. Like the English proverb, *"When in Rome, do as the Romans do"*, when in Santorini or any of the Greek Islands, do as the Greeks do.

You also want to come prepared to either pay for the whole meal or to graciously allow someone else cover the entire bill, contrary to the "Going Dutch" tradition of paying your own way in many cultures. Splitting the check is considered a cheap move and comes second on the list of faux pas right after ordering for yourself while in company. You will get your turn on a later day. Generosity and a big appetite are the only table manners required in Greece.

Santorini

***

Katherine and Jack arrived at the hotel at half past ten; greeted by Nikos and Theodora who were just starting their dinner out in the courtyard. Since sneaking into her room was impossible, Katherine accepted their invitation to join them and nibble something before going to bed. Just as soon as she sat, Theodora brought a shawl and placed it over Katherine's shoulders.

What started as a nibble ended up being a meal consisting of a couple of bites from a dozen deliciously prepared vegetarian dishes. Katherine was at first quiet and polite, but that didn't last as she became more comfortable with the Greek etiquette, and soon she was conversing as loudly as Jack, Theodora, and Nikos were.

The meal ended at around midnight, and Katherine helped Theodora clear the table, then the old couple retired, leaving Jack and Katherine sitting alone. There was a chill in the air, and Jack went to his room and brought a jacket and a bottle of cognac.

"Sorry, I don't have the proper cognac snifters," Jack apologized.

"These ones are just fine," Katherine said as he placed two shot glasses on the table. "My God, I'm full."

"You'll get used to it," Jack said, pouring two shots of cognac and handing one to Katherine.

"*Yiamas*," she said with a shy smile, trying her best to impress him with her lingo.

"*Yiamas*," Jack replied with a charming smile. "You're a fast learner."

"I have a good teacher," she replied sweetly. The starlight caught the sparkle in her shining eyes as she glanced at Jack. "I thought you went up to bring your pipe."

"My pipe?"

"All writers have pipes, don't they?"

Jack laughed at her joke.

"It's such a cliché," he commented. "It's all posing. It has nothing to do with writing."

"I thought it helped with the inspiration process."

"I never smoked and probably never will."

"So then what inspires you?" Katherine asked.

Her voice was so soft and sweet, and he could tell that she was genuinely curious to learn more about him and not just making idle conversation. As she did earlier, she clung to every word that he spoke and anticipated the next, and that made him feel so significant and influential, but more than that, he felt the honesty and purity in her soul as she listened intently.

"Everything," he replied, only to receive a slight frown from Katherine at his vague answer. "Life is full of inspirations."

"I mean your character. . . Annie, I think?" Katherine continued, and Jack nodded his approval. "She is brave, smart, young, and sexy all at the same time. I mean, is that how you like your women?"

"It's how women like their role models to be."

"Probably the ones who buy your books."

"All twelve million of them," Jack said and paused. "Including you," he bragged.

"I borrowed mine from a friend," Katherine said and laughed. "I knew that one day I would meet you and you would give me an autographed copy of all your books."

"Cheater."

"Tell that to your Annie. In every book, she sleeps with half a dozen different men."

"Now that was for the male readers," Jack said and laughed.

"You sure know your audience. Tell me, how did this writing thing start?"

"Was that lightning?" Jack asked as he saw a light flash to his right.

Then they both heard a rumble of thunder over the caldera.

"You just got your answer. Now I want mine," Katherine said, urging him to tell her his story.

Jack was asked this question at least once a week, and over the years, he had developed three different answers: one that meant "Go away, I don't want to tell you", and a second one that meant "I will give you the watered down version so that you will stop asking me". The third and least used variation that he was about to share with Katherine meant "I like you, and I want to spend as much time as I can with you".

Jack's fascination with writing started at a very early age. His father noticed his talent for storytelling and his passion for books and used to encourage him to read. In one of his rare interviews, Jack said that he even used to read the home appliance instruction manuals and even raid the medicine cabinet for the precautions and directions of use leaflets when he was out of conventional reading material.

He started writing at the age of twelve, and his first book was about a boy who went around helping the police solve crimes. At the age of sixteen, the idea of a female detective came to his mind, and when he started writing, he turned her into a private investigator. It was this character for whom he had become most well-known and who had afforded him his current lifestyle.

At first, he wrote using his own name. He sent his first book to a series of publishers, from whom he was still awaiting approval to this day. In college, he chose computer science as his major, and for a while, ditched writing prose for writing code. He graduated and was almost immediately snatched up by a Fortune 500 software company.

In the late nineties, he went to work for one of the internet companies whose business flourished and had an extremely promising and lucrative future. He moved to Silicon Valley and was given stock options that, in a matter of months, were worth tens of millions of dollars. His dream of early retirement was soon to be realized before his thirtieth birthday.

Soon after, however, the internet bubble burst, and all the green leaves in his high-rise corner office turned brown. He was left without a job, and the millions of stocks he held were worth a little less than a one-way, coach-class ticket back to New York City. He reluctantly moved back home with his parents, and to add to his misfortune, his dad passed away one month later.

One day, he was watching a rerun of one of his favorite childhood TV shows, *Remington Steele*. Almost immediately, he started writing again. He revisited the book he had written in his younger days and made some changes to it and sent it to an agent. Six weeks shy of his unemployment benefits running out, he received a call from his agent, informing him that a publisher made a bid on his book and was ready to give him an advance for the next two books in the series.

"And the rest, as they say, is history,"

Jack punctuated the end of his story by leaning back in his chair and folding his hands over his chest.

"Impressive," Katherine replied, feeling truly touched by his story and sympathetic about the hardships he had faced. "How about the women in your life? All three hundred and sixty five of them?"

"Does that number include the one who fell off the donkey?"

"Smart answer, Mr. Steele."

"Now your turn."

A few drops of rain were falling now and then as Jack was telling his story, but as soon as he finished and wanted Katherine to tell him her story, the skies opened and the rain started pouring. She stole a glance again at the caldera, whose waters now had turned deep and mysterious shades of indigo, midnight blue, and black. Just then another bolt of lightning arced through the night sky, igniting the water's surface with silvery brilliance.

"Rain check?" Katherine asked, smiling as she stood up and covering her hair with the shawl Theodora gave her and started walking towards her room.

Close Your Eyes and Jump

Jack was about to leave the house at around ten when he heard a knock on the door. He opened it and saw Katherine standing there. She looked lovely in the morning sun and didn't seem to realize he had opened the door because she was looking away and admiring the flowers that were blossoming near the door. She was wearing a tan sleeveless dress that fell nearly to her ankles and blew softly in the breeze. It was a simple cut, but it accentuated her lean figure, and she had one hand in her hair. Jack was amused at her distraction, and then she turned and smiled when he cleared his throat.

"I knocked on the other door, and a very sleepy German guy opened for me," she said with the blush of her cheeks the same shade of pink as the bougainvillea beside the door. "*Kalimera.*"

"He came in early this morning," Jack said. "He must have thought what a beautiful morning it was once he saw you, and good morning to you too. Please come in."

"Oh, you sure know how to make a girl smile," she said. "He wasn't too pleased, though, when he saw me like this."

Jack frowned, confused because he thought she looked perfect. She walked in, still blushing, and spun around so he could see what she was referring to. A round hairbrush was somehow stuck in her long wavy hair. It looked just like a Halloween prop, without the blood. Katherine held it with her hand so that it wouldn't pull her hair out or get tangled any more than it already was. Jack couldn't stop himself from laughing at the rat's nest she had somehow worked into her hair around the brush.

"I could just die from embarrassment right now," Katherine sighed. "I went to Theodora for help, but neither she nor Nikos is there, although the reception door is unlocked."

"They went to Kamari. An acquaintance died last night, and they have to attend the funeral," Jack explained. "It's on the eastern side of the island. They will most likely stay there til evening."

"Sorry to hear that," Katherine said with a look of concern on her face. "This can't stay up here till evening," she added, referring to the brush in her hair.

"It would be fun though. You never know; it might become the next big thing in fashion."

"Not cool, Steele, not cool at all."

"Don't worry. I'll help you get it out," Jack said, pointing to a chair. "Take a seat."

Katherine turned to go to the chair and saw the wall of books that Jack had in his room. Instead of sitting down, she walked towards it. Jack, in the meantime, was getting something from a box. He took it out and walked towards Katherine, who was now standing directly in front of the immense wall-to-wall bookcase. She was amazed at the sheer volume of books he had accumulated and on so many varied subjects.

"Anything you would like to borrow?" he asked.

"All of them."

"Then you better move in here," he said with a smile.

"Men!"

"Can't blame a guy for trying."

He held up in front of his face the scissors that he had been holding behind his back, grinned, then opened and closed the blades menacingly. As soon as Katherine saw them, she shouted and moved away from him, putting both hands on her hair to protect herself.

"Oh no you don't!" she shrieked. Don't you dare come near me with those!"

"Relax! I was just messing with you," Jack said and reached for a price tag dangling from her dress and cut it off.

"First time I've worn it," she said, blushing a little. "Thank you, but you really scared me."

"Now go sit down and stop being a little girl."

It took a great deal of patience and maneuvering to detangle the brush with the least damage, but Jack enjoyed the half hour he spent in her thick, lush hair. He tried to keep it "all business", but her hair smelled like coconut, and from time to time, he leaned closer to her only to sniff the delicious aroma. He had a hard time being this closely intimate with her and wanted to nuzzle his nose into the softness of her hair as he smoothed and caressed it, taking extra care to not pull or break too many strands.

Being this close to any woman made him happy, and Katherine was one very attractive woman that any man would be happy to be close to. Her feeling towards Jack was almost the same; after all, he was an attractive man. He was also smart, fun to be with, and most of all, unpretentious. His sense of humor was a little bit scary though, as she remembered the blades of the scissors flash in front of his face.

She felt her whole body warming up once he put both hands in her hair. She couldn't have predicted how weak she would feel once his hand rubbed against the back of her neck and was glad that she was sitting down. His face was too close for comfort too, and though she was a bit uncomfortable, for a moment, she wished that his lips would plant a kiss on her neck. She closed her eyes, dismissing all those thoughts from her head, and prayed that her hair would be free from his hands as soon as possible.

If she had been able to see him, she would have seen the soft smile that played around his lips as he worked, but she could only feel the careful, loving touch that he used, and from time to time, she would feel his hand brush against her skin or feel the heat of his body radiate onto her. She wanted to escape from this invasion of her personal space, yet running away was the last thing she wanted to do.

"And done," he said.

She let out a sigh of relief and thanked him. She was sad to see that she lost a few hairs in the process, but it was a small price to pay, considering her options if this hadn't worked. She used his mirror to fix her hair and went back to the wall of books.

Jack, in the meantime, left the room for a couple of minutes as she perused the shelves. Katherine turned around once she smelled the freshly brewed coffee. She saw Jack holding two small cups on a tray with two glasses of water.

"We never had that coffee," he said as he placed the tray on a small table.

"It smells great. Same as Turkish coffee," Katherine said, and Jack opened his eyes wide.

Greek coffee is known for its foamy top and strong brew. The foam is caused by the shape of the pot that it is made in. The Greeks call the pot *briki*, and it was traditionally made of copper. You have to use the right ratio of water to coffee to get the best results. You should also never forget to drink cold water after you finish your coffee; it will allow the flavor to linger on your palate while washing away the bitterness. Jack had perfected the process over the years and was very proud to serve his guests who usually commented positively on his coffee. The only thing that you should avoid while commenting on Greek coffee, which Katherine now learned, is calling it Turkish coffee.

"Oh! Bitter!" Katherine said after taking one sip.

"Sorry. I will get you some sugar. I take it like this and usually forget that other people have different taste."

The coffee tasted better after putting three spoons of white sugar in it. Greek coffee cups are very small, and Jack commented that Katherine should have poured some coffee in the sugar jar instead of the opposite. She didn't care for his comment, and the girl loved the taste of sugar, no matter what anyone said.

"I'm sorry for interrupting your morning. I'm sure you had better plans than setting my poor hair free?"

"I was going down to the port. I needed to give someone a package to take it with him to Heraklion in Crete."

"Don't let me keep you," she said and started to stand up.

"He will be there all day. Finish your coffee first."

"Just don't take the donkey," she said and laughed.

"I will take the cable car down and walk back up," he said. "I walk up and down the stairs every morning at six, but today it was still raining, and I wasn't in the mood to get wet."

"You're an early riser," she commented. "I prefer waking up at around... now."

"I wake up to write in the morning while my mind is sharp and uncluttered."

"Lucky you," she said and stood up.

"If you are not doing anything, you can come with me to the port, and we can take a tour of the island after that," he offered, hoping to prolong the time in her company.

"I was going to do just that," she said. "Having a guide will make the experience even better."

Katherine was also excited to spend some time with Jack. She had traveled to many places and met people from all over the world. One thing she learned was to be careful of strangers, especially the nicer ones, because the creepy ones are already known, but the nice ones might be hiding a secret agenda. Jack was one of the genuinely nice ones. She would never let her guard down around him, but so far he proved to be trustworthy and dependable.

Jack went to the kitchenette with the empty cups while Katherine further fixed her hair and looked around his room. His bed was neatly made, and that was rare to see in a man's room. Even the pillows were fluffed and perfectly aligned at the head of the bed. A book lay on his couch with a bookmark in its beginnings. *Looks like he just started reading it,* Katherine thought. He had a small TV facing the couch, something she didn't have in her room, and she didn't care that she didn't. She didn't miss it one bit.

In front of the window overlooking the courtyard and a magnificent view of the caldera was a table with only a vintage typewriter on it and a stack of paper. She was intrigued and walked towards it then stood looking down on the keys. It looked so beautiful and romantic, and a little bit complicated. Katherine had never used a typewriter; by the time she needed to type her school assignments, her dad let her use his Apple Macintosh Plus. Later in her senior year in school, he bought her a Macintosh LC.

Katherine noticed the iMac in the corner of the room with a 17-inch LCD screen and thought how much things had changed since the Macintosh Plus and its tiny 9-inch monochrome screen. Well, that was 1988, and now it was 2004. She looked curiously at the stack of papers on one side of the table. She put her hand on the paperweight covering them and lifted it.

"I wouldn't do that if I was you," Jack's voice came from behind her.

"Oh!" she cried, startled by his voice then dropped the paperweight to the floor. She winced as it bounced off her foot first before hitting the floor.

"I didn't mean to frighten you," Jack said, coming close to her and guiding her into a chair.

"I must be the clumsiest woman you have ever met; I keep

falling down, sticking things in my hair, dropping paperweights on my foot."

Jack started laughing as he picked up the paper weight off the floor and put it back on top of the pile of papers. He bent down on one knee and took Katherine's sandal off and examined her foot. She was so embarrassed and yet she liked the care he was giving her.

"Wiggle your toes," he ordered. He examined them and said, "They all work fine."

"Will I ever walk again doctor?" she asked with an innocent voice.

"And run the marathon," Jack said, putting her sandal back on and standing up.

"Sorry, I didn't mean to pry."

"Don't be. You must be wondering why someone who's specialized in computer science and who owns a computer is typing on a sixty-year old typewriter."

That never occurred to her; she thought all good writers used typewriters, the same as she thought that they all smoked pipes. She was just curious, and her curiosity almost killed her toes, but since he gave her a better excuse, she used it.

"Exactly," she said.

"Come. I'll tell you on our way down to the port."

Jack took a small case from underneath the table and walked with Katherine out of his room. She made a stop in her room, and when she came out, she carried a large shoulder bag and was wearing a wide-brimmed hat with oversized sunglasses. She looked like a movie star from another era. He thought the only thing missing was the scarf that should be streaming behind her, then he caught a glimpse of one sticking out of her bag.

"This will double as an umbrella, in case you were wondering," she said, indicating the comically large hat that both of them could practically fit under, and he just smiled.

***

The view from the gondola that ran from the island's highest elevation to the port below was one of the best views you could have of the island. It took Katherine's breath away as they descended in the cable car down the cliff side. It was a dazzling view, and the vivid blue sea that was open before them was indescribable. No matter how many times she saw the clusters of houses and the wall that ran along the winding steps, it made her think of castles or a fortress and made the scene look like a fairytale. Seeing from above the infinite maze of steps that wound down the cliff made her realize just how strong and resilient Santorini's residents must be.

Katherine watched with amazement as Jack narrated the three-minute trip down to the shore. He didn't mind her close proximity and was glad to see her enjoying herself in his company; he loved her enthusiasm for the island, which he had come to take pride in as his home. Santorini provided the scenery, and Katherine provided the sweetness.

"I loved it!" she shouted, grabbing his arms with both hands as they dismounted. "Let's do it again."

"We will. First let me check this in," he said, referring to the case he was holding.

"What is this anyways?"

"A nine-millimeter gun with a silencer."

Katherine's eyes widened and she felt the blood drain from her face as she remembered the glint of the scissor blades and his devilish grin as he held them.

"Really?!"

Jack let out a hearty laugh and wiped tears of laughter from his eyes.

"No! But I enjoyed the look on your face."

"You almost got me there," she confessed. "Seriously, what's in it?"

"A typewriter I bought a couple of weeks ago. It needs maintenance, and the only guy I know who can fix this model is in Heraklion, so I am shipping it to him."

The ferry port looked rather small. There were no ships docked there at the moment, so it looked almost deserted. Jack went into a small office as she waited outside looking in. She was disappointed to see that he was greeted by a rather clingy woman who Katherine thought acted too friendly with Jack, very attractive too.

After kissing him on both cheeks, which appeared to be very normal to her, she started touching him as she spoke, laying her hand on his arm and moving to his chest, and leaned forward as she talked to him. Jack didn't seem to mind that at all but also didn't seem to respond to it as if he was trying to be tactful. Katherine wondered if at some point he was seeing that woman. *He was single and handsome and nice and famous, why wouldn't she want to date him?*

"We're done," Jack said once he came out, cutting short Katherine's thoughts.

"Great."

"That was Doctor Vasilis's daughter; I give her daughter English lessons."

"Oh! I never had the chance to thank him. Do you think I should?"

"I can always give you his number or you can go with me to his house on Monday afternoon."

"It's his birthday?" Katherine asked jokingly.

Jack laughed at Katherine's joke. He loved the way she mixed it effortlessly into a conversation. She would make a great poker player or a spy, the way she could keep a straight face.

"I give Eleni, his granddaughter, lessons twice a week,

Mondays and Thursdays." Jack explained. To sweeten the deal to lure her to come along, he added, "I also use his swimming pool."

"This entire sea is not enough for you?"

"I don't swim in salt water. It gives me a rash."

"Too bad because I thought we could go swimming today."

"The water is still too cold," Jack said with a shiver as he imagined Katherine in a bikini.

"I'm from San Francisco. The water is always cold."

"The coldest winter I ever spent…" Jack started to say.

"…was a summer in San Francisco," Katherine said, finishing the quote. "Mark Twain."

"Not bad," Jack commented. "Now what?"

"Now you show a girl a good time, Mr. Steele."

***

Jack wanted to rent a car, and Katherine loved the idea of a scooter, although she was wearing a dress and had her oversized hat and bag. Scooters are nice to ride, but they are too bouncy, so they compromised. Katherine won the argument, that is. Jack didn't have the heart to disappoint her, so what the lady wants, the lady gets.

They started with a tour of the island with Jack driving and Katherine sitting sideways behind him. The one-hour trip resulted in Katherine's hat flying off more than ten times and innocently flashing her panties to tourists and locals a dozen times as the wind filled her dress and blew it over her head, but all was fun for both of them.

The best part for Jack was to hear her giggles in his ears and to feel her tight hold around him. Several times she pressed into him to shout in his ear over the loud sound of the scooter's high pitched engine. The hair would stand on the back of his neck every time her lips accidently brushed over it. He also *accidentally on purpose* took a few turns a little too sharply and slowed abruptly, only to feel her squeeze him a little tighter, and he sped away a little faster than he should have from time to time, only to hear her squeals of delight.

They ended up exploring the ruins of Ancient Thera, strategically located on a rocky ridge overlooking the whole island. Katherine took out her camera and started taking pictures of her surroundings. Jack then took pictures of her in different places, posing as a Hellenic princess of an ancient civilization.

Katherine pretended to perform in the ancient theater and walk in the Agora, the main square. She visited the Imperial family in their private chambers and prayed for the mighty god Apollo. They both had so much fun that to the few tourist onlookers present there, they were the lovers who everyone wished to be.

They left Thera around two and headed to Oia, recommended by Jack as the best view of the caldera. It is a small village located in the northern part of the island of Santorini, right at the top of the crescent. All of its homes, churches, shops, restaurants and hotels are built on a steep slope overlooking the caldera. Between them, there are narrow passages converging into a central square.

Katherine and Jack parked the scooter and walked around the village. Almost all of its houses were white with blue windows. All of its churches had blue roofs with cupolas. The village was absolutely charming and amazing, and Katherine told Jack that if she ever decided to call a place home she would come and live in Oia.

They started walking down from Oia towards a beach called Amoudi. After ten minutes of walking, the path became a little bit tricky, so Jack offered Katherine his hand, and they walked closely hand in hand the rest of the way. A few minutes later, they spotted someone running and jumping off of a rock. Moments later, someone else jumped, and then a third.

"They are jumping into the water!" Katherine squealed and jumped in place then ran, pulling Jack behind her.

They arrived at the rock three minutes later and both looked down. It was high above the water, and the three guys who jumped were now on a small island very close to the shore. Katherine didn't skip a beat; she took off her hat and gave it to Jack.

"Don't tell me you're gonna jump," Jack said.

"You bet I am!"

"You're wearing a dress."

"I'll take it off," she said, and when she saw Jack's eyes pop out, she said, "I brought my bikini with me." She paused for a second then said, "That's what the big bag is for, handsome. Now turn."

Jack turned around as Katherine put her bag down and opened it. First, she discreetly took off her panties and put them in the bag and took out the bikini bottoms and put them on. Then she lowered the top of her dress, took off her bra, and put on the bikini top. Finally, she completely took her dress off, stuffed it her bag, and hooked it on Jack's shoulder.

"Wanna join me?" she asked as he turned around and looked at her.

Jack paused, but he wasn't thinking. He was just admiring her beauty. Her sleek, sexy body only covered with a few inches of fabric stood a few feet in front of him. Katherine read the lust in Jack's eyes and blushed. She turned around and took off her sandals.

The guys on the small island of *Agios Nikolaos* saw her and started cheering and urging her to jump. She never looked back and ran and jumped into the water, holding her legs close to her chest in mid-air. She went down with a splash, and the three guys cheered enthusiastically again as she emerged. Soon Jack realized why they were cheering that much. Katherine had lost her bikini top in the jump.

"Don't look!" Katherine shouted up at Jack.

"What do you want me to do?"

"Turn around and tell me how do I get to the beach?"

"If you want to flash your tits to a couple of Greek families with children and all, go to your left. If not, there is a patch on your right with no one on it," Jack shouted down to her while looking the other way.

"Can you get my things and meet me there?"

"Like a good errand boy, I will, ma'am!"

"You're adorable! Don't forget my sandals!"

Five minutes later, Jack was at sea level. Katherine was sitting in the middle of a patch of sand tucked between the rocks. She heard his steps and turned her head around while one arm was across her breasts.

"You're a life saver," she said. "Now keep it there and turn around."

"It's better that you change facing the rocks."

"Let's switch places," she said and stood up, but Jack didn't move.

He stood captivated, looking at her. Her shimmering blue eyes, her beautiful wet brown hair, her slender body, and her sweet smile all called him to look at her. She was embarrassed by the way she felt his eyes wandering over every inch of her body yet loved every blink of his eyes. His look was not only of pure desire but of longing and admiration.

Katherine looked long into Jack's eyes and walked towards him, her right arm still covering her breasts. She stood only a few inches away from him, uncomfortably close yet not nearly close enough. She leaned forward and stood on her toes, her lips almost touching his ear.

"She stood naked in front of him, his eyes lusting with desire..." she whispered.

Jack didn't move a muscle and swallowed hard, waiting for what she would say next. She came closer and put her free hand on his then said:

"...Now give me my clothes back!"

Jack was expecting much more, expected the scene to progress to at least a kiss, but he stood in shock as Katherine snatched the bag from his hand and walked behind him. Though he was surprised, he could only smile as he looked at the blue sea in front of him. Katherine put her dress back on turned around, his back still to her. She came from behind him and slipped her arms around his waist and gave him a kiss on the cheek.

A Family Matter

"Now what?" Jack said to himself when he heard Katherine screaming from her room.

Sundays on Santorini are absolutely magnificent, where a divine tranquility settles on the island, and almost all fifteen thousand islanders flock to the tiny churches balanced on the cliffs. If you had a late night like Jack did, you would be awakened in the morning by a symphony of hundreds of church bells ringing all at once in different tones. Jack loved the sound, and on a few occasions, he accompanied Nikos and Theodora to church.

It's the best place to put your eye on a bride, Theodora used to tell him. He, however, was there for the enchanting Byzantine chants that reverberated through the church. The frankincense that was burned uplifted him as he breathed in the clean aroma. It cleared his mind and set his soul at ease, and then he was able to put his thoughts onto paper with more eloquence and clarity than before.

Although his faultless internal clock woke him up at six, today he didn't feel like getting out of bed. After their beach escapade yesterday, he and Katherine hiked back to Oia, found a nice restaurant with a view, and sat there for a couple of hours. They talked over a nice dinner and shared two bottles of wine. After, they went back to the hotel, changed their clothes, and went down to a tavern. The last thing he remembered was that Katherine was teaching him a Greek dance and he was failing miserably but loving the lesson.

They walked back home at around two, and they each went to their own room. Jack passed out almost immediately and slept in his clothes then changed into his boxer shorts when he woke up a couple hours later. Now it was almost eleven, and he was lying in bed, thinking about a scene in his book, when Katherine's screams interrupted his line of thought.

He bolted across the room and opened his door, and the screams became louder. He ran back inside, put his jeans on, and grabbed the first weapon he could find. The screams were coming from her room, so he ran barefoot and bare-chested down the stairs to rescue her from what certainly must be an intruder. He kicked open the door and barged in holding a broom like a gladiator holding his sword two thousand years ago.

Jack burst into laughter as soon as he saw Katherine standing on her bed wearing a bathrobe and holding a flashlight in her hand. She was pointing it at a chicken that was standing in the middle of the room. Judging from the state of the room with clothing and furniture strewn about, both girls were running around before the standoff occurred.

"Stop laughing, and get this animal out of here!" Katherine screamed and started shrieking again.

"It's a bird! And what's that flashlight for? Are you trying to zap it?"

"A bird, a fish, what's the difference? Just get it out! Please!"

Jack laughed again, and as soon as he walked towards the chicken, it started going in circles and then started running around the room, flapping its wings and squawking. Katherine's screams returned, and she started jumping on her bed.

Then Katherine dropped the flashlight and picked up a pillow. Jack caught the hen and held her in his arms. She immediately calmed down and started clucking softly as he pet her smooth, soft head. He walked towards Katherine, holding the chicken trying to frighten her. He pushed it toward her, taunting her, enjoying her squeals and screams. She started hitting him with the pillow until the chicken slipped from his hands and ran out the door. The pillow suddenly burst, and a blizzard of feathers filled the room. Jack finally was able to grab Katherine's wrists to get her to stop pummeling him with her small fists.

Both of them were covered with feathers then looked towards the door when they heard someone clear their throat loudly. Five people stood there blocking the entrance, all wearing Sunday clothes: Theodora, Nikos, Yiorgos, Maria and Maria's ten-year old nephew, Alexandros. They started to laugh all at once, to the embarrassment of Katherine and Jack.

"I will get you a new pillow," Theodora said before she dismissed everyone and closed the door.

Jack was still holding Katherine's wrists, both of them breathing heavily from the chase. Her satin bathrobe was clinging to her body, and the tiny white feathers stuck to her hair like freshly fallen snowflakes. He softened his grip as he looked deep into her eyes. He lowered his hands and slipped them around her waist and eased her off the bed. She slowly slid down his naked muscled torso.

As their bodies connected, so did their minds, switching to the same wave length. Their eyes met, inviting their lips. Accepting the invitation, their lips met for the first time. Shyly and softly at first, then like very old lovers finding each other after a long time apart. Their hungry lips parted, allowing their tongues to have a taste.

A sudden knock on the door disrupted their kiss.

"Coffee in five," Theodora's voice called.

Their lips parted but their bodies stayed close, their eyes staring, still wanting more. Jack set Katherine's feet on the floor, and she only then realized that she had held in his arms in mid air for the length of the kiss. Her feet settled on a bed of soft feathers, and she looked up at him longingly.

"I probably should go," Jack said, still holding her tightly.

"Me too," she said. "I mean, you should go, then I go out and have coffee," she stuttered, her brain still processing the kiss.

***

It wasn't after Theodora's insistence and threatening to knock down the door that Katherine had the guts to come out of the room. She was so embarrassed, and her face almost matched her red dress. Everybody was out, and they were all talking, arguing and laughing, all in Greek. All she could think about was that her recent disaster was the center of attention.

"Are they talking about me?" she asked Jack once she sat next to him.

"Yes, and you should be glad that they forgot all about the donkey and the fall," he replied. He was fibbing, of course, but he enjoyed tormenting her.

"Because now they have the chicken to talk about," she muttered as she covered her face with both hands.

Theodora came around and poured fresh coffee into her cup.

"This is *vari glykos,* means very sweet. Made it especially for you because very sweet girls like their coffee very sweet," Theodora said and gave a very embarrassed Katherine a kiss on the cheek.

"I'm very happy with my *metrios* wife," Nikos said.

"Consider yourself lucky, old man," Theodora answered playfully.

"What's *metrios*?" Katherine asked Jack discreetly.

"Medium sweet."

Traditionally, on Sunday after church, Greek families gather together for lunch. The children play, and the parents and grandparents discuss family matters and catch up. Women would be usually busy preparing the food while the men talked politics and fought over the best method to fire the charcoal for grilling. During Lent, though, all the food is vegetarian so no need for the charcoal, and the men's discussion was only about politics.

Katherine was invited by the ladies into the kitchen for an improvised lesson in Greek cuisine. She was assured that there wouldn't be any chicken present, dead or alive. She was embarrassed because of the joke made on her account but took it lightly.

"Jack is very sweet," Maria said with a wink as she was cutting the tomatoes into thin wedges.

"He is?" Katherine wondered with his taste still lingering on her tongue.

"Without him, I wouldn't be here or even getting married in three weeks."

"Really?"

"I'm a dentist, and one day Jack came in to have his teeth cleaned," Maria began. As a side note, she added, "You Americans take good care of your teeth, by the way," then continued. "Yes, where was I? So he wanted to pay me by credit card, and I told him I don't have a machine. So he called his banker and told him to send someone. Half an hour later, Yiorgos was in my office to set me up with a POS terminal."

"Very interesting story," Katherine said, impressed by Jack's generosity.

"Jack just looked at us and said, 'You two should be together'."

"Pass me the salt, sweetheart," Theodora asked Katherine,

who spent half a minute looking for the salt before Theodora found it and took it herself.

"So Yiorgos used to work at a bank?"

"Still does. The bar is his afternoon hobby. He inherited it from his late uncle."

An hour later, the food was ready, and they all sat at the table. It was the most interesting hotel experience Katherine had ever had. She felt like she was an exchange student or even a visitor of some relatives in a distant country. It was very sweet, like the coffee she drank earlier and like the lips she kissed before that.

All through lunch, the talking and arguing didn't stop. Almost all of the conversation was in Greek, but Jack translated most of the important parts to Katherine, who was enjoying him leaning close to her every now and then. She blushed when Maria made a comment about the two of them.

"Jack and Katherine, you two should be together."

Everybody stopped talking and eating. Jack didn't know what to say, and neither did Katherine. Then everybody was saved by Alexandros.

"Who is more intelligent, white or black chicken?"

"Both are dumb to me," Katherine answered.

"No, you have to choose one," Alexandros objected.

"White one?"

"Wrong answer," Alexandros said. "The black chicken is the most intelligent because she can lay white eggs while the white chicken can't lay black eggs."

***

"A fish. . .No. . .a dolphin," Theodora guessed, looking into Maria's coffee cup.

The ladies were having some coffee and fortune reading after clearing the table and washing the dishes. Jack and Yiorgos went down to open the bar, and Nikos was taking a well-deserved nap. It was almost five, and all combined, it had been a whole six hours of having coffee and making food, eating, having more coffee, and the whole time, no one stopped talking. It was somehow tiring for Katherine, but she enjoyed every single moment of it, except, of course, the part where they teased her about the chicken. She would prefer to forget that embarrassment instead of being constantly reminded of it.

Eleni, Dr. Vasilis's granddaughter, came to play with Alexandros. She was a sweet girl, *not like her clingy mother*, Katherine thought. Her mother who kept leaning into Jack and touching him everywhere while she spoke to him. She wondered to herself why that annoyed her so much. He was a free man he could do whatever he wanted and be touched and leaned into by whomever he wanted. Absorbed in her thoughts, she pressed her lips together and bit her lower lip.

I wish he would kiss me again.

"Sweetheart? Wake up," Maria said gently, poking her in the arm and snapping her back to reality. "It's your turn."

Theodora picked up Katherine's cup that was inverted on the saucer and turned it over. Looking into the cup to study the dregs of coffee that remained, she suddenly gasped then covered her eyes with her other hand, unable to bear what she saw.

"What is it?" Katherine asked, startled and worried about Theodora's reaction. "What's wrong with my cup?"

Katherine's heart was beating fast as she anxiously leaned towards the old woman. Her mind raced as Theodora gave her a long, serious look. She wondered what the coffee grounds could possibly reveal to replace Theodora's normally placid expression with one so grim.

"Too many chicken flying around," Theodora finally said.

"Oh!" Katherine cried, covering her face with both hands as Theodora and Maria both started laughing.

Theodora leaned and took Katherine's hands off of her blushing face then kissed her on her forehead. She sat back then held up the cup again and examined it carefully. She glanced at Katherine and looked back into the cup.

"Looks like there was an earthquake because I see two broken pillars," Theodora began with a serious tone. "I see a boat...and a girl just like you standing on it. Her back is turned to the destruction."

Katherine and Maria listened attentively.

"I see a handsome man."

"Wow," Maria said while Katherine was unable to speak.

"Here...see for yourself,"

Theodora showed the cup to Maria and Katherine, who curiously leaned forward. "The man is looking at the girl on the boat...behind him...there are old ruins...and leaves with a letter on each leaf."

Then Theodora looked closer and smiled.

"You...I mean the girl...and the man are both connected,"

Theodora leaned forward and showed them the two figures from each side of the cup connected in the bottom of the picture of the broken pillars. Katherine wasn't even sure exactly what she was looking at; to her, it still only looked like coffee grounds clinging to the coffee cup.

"What does this all mean?" Maria asked.

"In three...could be three days...or three weeks...or three months my dear Katherina, you will get engaged," Theodora announced.

"No way!" Katherine objected. "I'm not even dating,"

"I only say what I see," Theodora said with a tone of finality. "If the cup says you will get engaged, then you will get engaged.

When I was a little girl, our neighbor read my cup for me and told me that I will get married young and the man I marry would have a mole next his…"

"Oh! No, no, no!" Maria shouted shyly. "Don't say it!"

Theodora and Katherine laughed.

"You are marrying my son, you shouldn't blush like this," Theodora said then quickly excused herself. "I want to go lie down for a while and leave you girls to talk."

***

Almost twenty people were gathered around the entrance of Alexandrino. Jack and Yiorgos arrived at the bar and found that the lock had been smashed. A local police officer, who happened to be passing by, secured the area and offered to assist them in case the burglar was still inside.

They cautiously followed behind the officer, and to their surprise, there were half a dozen teenagers inside, a couple of them passed out on the floor amidst some emptied bottles. The others were slumped in their chairs, obviously very drunk. The sound of the door opening startled the kids, and the ones who were able jumped and scattered, clumsily trying to get away. Their only escape was through the front door and past the three angry men who were blocking it. In the end, after a small scuffle, only one made it out and disappeared between a labyrinth of narrow paths.

In the commotion, the teenagers knocked down a cabinet holding a few wine bottles and two or three dozen glasses. The floor was filled with broken glass and pools of white and red wine mixing together. What made Yiorgos sad, though, was that his collection of vinyl records had fallen off the shelves and scattered over the floor. Some of these records were priceless, and some were autographed by very famous Greek artists.

Phone calls to the kids' parents were made, and Yiorgos and Jack started to pick up the records in an effort to save them. The police officer was waking up the kids who had passed out. Soon, people started coming in, and then the parents came. After a couple of slaps, lots of shouting, and a half-hour negotiation with Yiorgos about the costs, the matter was solved amicably without pressing charges.

"What happened?" Katherine shouted as she entered the bar. She looked around at the damage and was shocked that someone on this otherwise tranquil island was capable of such a thing.

"Some kids broke in and got drunk," Jack said as he swept the broken glass away. "Watch your step," he added as he darted across to guide her through the debris.

"You know, this is the second time today I have seen you holding a broom in your hand," Katherine said with a smile. "How can I help?"

"Well, you can sort out the records alphabetically," he suggested, pointing to the records piled on the table.

Katherine talked to Yiorgos for a couple of minutes and told him that Maria was outside talking to her aunt. Yiorgos went out, and Katherine went to the table, happy to lend a hand but then stood there and stared at records. She picked up one record then another then another and then set them down again on the table.

"They are all in Greek," she said.

"That's the challenge," Jack said with a wink as he started to laugh.

He looked around and saw that the place was empty and the front door was closed. He stopped sweeping and walked towards Katherine. She looked up and saw him standing right in front of her. Involuntarily, her lips parted a little, and her heart beat increased as the blood rushed to her blushing cheeks.

"Listen...about what happened this morning," Jack said softly.

She tried to avoid looking directly into his eyes as he leaned closer to her. She knew that if she did, she would lose all of the strength she had summoned to not kiss him. "I wanted to talk to you about it, but it was hard with all those people around us...I ..."

"It was in the heat of the moment," she said casually, interrupting him before he could finish. She struggled to maintain an air of nonchalance. "I totally understand. It's the same for me."

That wasn't what Jack wanted to say or at least it wasn't how he felt. It wasn't how Katherine felt either. That kiss changed something inside her, triggered a feeling that was buried deep and brought it to the surface. For him, Katherine wasn't just another girl who happened to be close so he kissed her. She didn't only make his blood rush, she made his heart come to life.

Katherine waited for Jack to say something else, but he didn't. Instead, he came closer to her, his eyes piercing hers. They were inches away from each other, their breath mixing together as it came out from between their eager lips. He wanted to kiss her, and she wanted it more. It would be their second heat of the moment kiss if they gave in to the urge.

Just as their lips were about to touch, Yiorgos and Maria barged in, and they quickly separated.

"Your aunt is just crazy to suggest such a thing," Yiorgos said, raising his voice.

"She's a woman from a different generation," Maria argued. "You can't blame her for thinking like that."

"You judge," Yiorgos said to Jack and Katherine, who were now standing two feet apart, looking at him and his fiancée and hoping to avoid getting in the middle of something.

"I will tell them," Maria interrupted. "My aunt, who's actually my dad's aunt and who's a million years old, suggested that the kids' parents bring them here and make them stand outside the bar facing the wall all day long so that they would be humiliated and become an example to all naughty teenagers."

Katherine and Jack didn't answer; they just stood there. What was on their mind wasn't the bar or the teens or Maria's aunt. What was on their mind was that kiss that almost happened, the flame that was smoldering and was suddenly doused before it could ignite. Their yearning hearts pounded in unison in their chests. Maria and Yiorgos were too involved in their discussion to realize they had interrupted something.

"I just don't want your aunt near our children with her old fashioned ideas," Yiorgos said. "That's it."

"Me neither," Maria said and leaned into Yiorgos who gave her a hug and a kiss.

Katherine and Jack were happy that they didn't get involved in what was supposed to be a family matter.

"So what are we doing here?" Maria asked Katherine.

"Well, I am supposed to sort these records, but they are all Greek to me."

***

The four of them opened a bottle of wine after they finished cleaning the bar and rearranging everything inside it. It was too late to open, so they decided to relax and spend some time together, just the four of them. It was almost eleven when they went back home after each telling a story from their childhood.

Maria was born on Santorini, and at the age of twelve, her family moved to the island of Crete and later to Athens. They visited their relatives and their old house a couple of times a year during holidays, and Maria spent most of her summer with her old friends and relatives on Santorini.

After graduating from college, she practiced dentistry for one year in Athens and then moved back to Santorini and opened her own clinic. It was so different for her since everybody here wanted to chat with her and ask about her parents. Some used to bring her food since her parents were still living in Athens. She loved the familial feeling and sense of community on the island.

Then Jack became her client, and he brought Yiorgos into her life, and because of him, she was now getting married. She had met Yiorgos a few times before, but they never spoke. The island was small enough such that everyone seemed a familiar face but too big to know them all personally.

Jack was born in Brooklyn, New York. His father was a police officer, and his mother was a homemaker. When he was growing up, he had a dog named Chad. All was wonderful until some guy named Chad moved into the neighborhood. Somehow Chad and Chad didn't get along together very well, and Chad the Dog used to go and do his business in Chad the Angry Guy's yard.

Later, Jack moved to Silicon Valley and became a VP of software development for an internet company. His company paid two million dollars for a 30-second spot during the Super Bowl game between the St. Louis Rams and the Tennessee Titans on January 30, 2000, then went bankrupt two months later. As Jack put it, "One night we were drinking Cristal Champagne from silver cups, and the next morning we were pawning our Rolex watches for food."

After moving back with his parents and nursing his bruised ego, he pulled himself out of his depression and published his first book then took a vacation to Greece in August 2001. He ended up in Santorini and loved it so much that he decided to stay. He wrote his second, third, and fourth books while on the island, and he was about to finish writing his fifth book without leaving the island for one single day.

Yiorgos knew about the controversy surrounding his birth at the age of twelve when one of the children in his school teased him about being Dr. Vasilis's son. He was devastated; he loved his mother more than anyone in the world. Things got worse when Theodora and Nikos had to answer to that kid's parents on why Yiorgos had given their son a broken nose. Yiorgos didn't want to say at first, but then he started crying and said what was on his mind.

Theodora acted very calmly, as if she expected it. Nikos was furious and couldn't believe that Yiorgos would accuse his own mother of infidelity. Theodora grabbed each one of them and put them in front of a mirror and ordered them to take their shirts off, revealing their identical birth marks. Yiorgos recalled exactly what she said:

"This is your evidence, and your second one is that you have the same exact fiery temper and hard headedness as your father...Now go do your homework."

Yiorgos finished his college studies in finance at the Aristotle University of Thessaloniki then came back home. He started work at a bank soon after, even though he received better offers from companies and financial institutions in Athens. He liked to stay close to his roots, and inheriting the bar after his uncle's death gave him a better reason to stay. When he met Maria, he was so happy that they shared the same strong family values, and thanks to Jack, they would share it for the rest of their lives.

Katherine was reluctant to talk at first, then after the urging of everybody who felt it unfair of her to "chicken out", she started to talk. She was born in Vancouver, Canada, where her parents were on vacation and thought that she wasn't due for three weeks more, demolishing her chances of becoming the first female President of the United States.

She lived all her life in San Francisco, and at the age of thirteen, her mom and dad got divorced; her mom later remarried a U.S. Marine Colonel. She rarely saw her mom because her new stepfather was stationed overseas and every couple of years was relocated from one place to another, leaving Katherine behind without a role model in her teen years. Her dad started his career as a cartoonist and then became one of the best known courtroom sketch artists on the West Coast.

She studied psychology at San Francisco State University and graduated summa cum laude. Her mother had flown in to see her graduate, and somehow the fire rekindled between her parents, and they got back together. Her mother filed for divorce from her Marine husband, and before Christmas that year, her parents remarried.

Neither Jack nor Katherine spoke about their love life. Maria and Yiorgos were curious to know but then Katherine said that it would be the subject for another day and they should call it a night. With her words, she saved both Jack and herself from divulging their painful pasts.

"Do you want us to accompany you home?" Yiorgos asked Jack and Katherine. "You never know, there might be a mad chicken running around," he joked.

Bed of Feathers

Jack walked hand in hand with Katherine back to the hotel. The sky was filled with twinkling stars, and the half-moon reflected on the water of the caldera. There was a chill in the air, and Jack slipped his arm around Katherine, who appreciated the warmth it gave her. She felt more than warmth; she felt the care that she craved for, the strong grip of his arm, and the softness of his touch. She felt her body relax and eased herself into him, trusting the security that he offered.

They arrived in front of her room then both paused silently. Katherine played with her keys in her pocket, but she didn't make a move to open her door. Jack stood quietly looking at the night sky and wished Katherine would invite him inside, but he was too much of a gentleman to suggest it. He turned to face her, and the simple light fixture above her door illuminated her face with a warm glow that shined into his eyes. She smiled and two soft dimples formed on her cheeks as she turned her eyes to look up at him. Time seemed to stop as they stood together, unsure of what the other wanted yet both hesitant to make their desire known.

"I would invite you in," Katherine said softly, finally breaking the silence. "But I have to clean up first."

"I can help you," he offered with a gentle smile playing around the corners of his mouth that she so much wanted to reach up to kiss. "Or check the room for you in case the chicken has returned."

Katherine had opened her mouth to speak when they both heard someone outside the main gate. The language was German, and there were two or three people outside, a distinctive male voice and another female voice. Katherine fished out her keys, and as soon as she unlocked her door, a German man stepped into the courtyard with one girl on each arm.

Katherine quickly opened the door and pushed Jack inside before she went in herself. They waited at the door as the man started to sing right outside her room. Jack stood closely behind Katherine at the window; she could feel the warmth of his body radiate onto hers as they both took a peek at the scene outside. The drunken man was swaying around while singing loudly and off-key in German as his female companions tried to guide him towards the stairs. A few minutes later, the three of them managed to make it up to the second floor then Katherine and Jack heard the door close but could still hear the muffled sounds of his singing and the girls giggling.

"I will have to stuff cotton balls in my ears," Jack commented as Katherine turned on the lights. "Someone is gonna be busy tonight."

"German songs all night long," Katherine said, fully aware that he was referring to the sounds of the threesome's lovemaking that would continue through the night.

Jack started laughing when she turned the lights on and he saw the state of Katherine's room. Little white feathers covered everything, including her bed. Embarrassed by it, she quickly covered his eyes with her hands. As she reached up to him, her body leaned into his, igniting again the spark of desire inside them both.

"Stop teasing me," she pleaded. "I didn't have time to clean up with all the coffee and food and people and stories."

"I didn't say anything!"

"Your eyes did. That's why I covered them," she said. "The eyes can say a lot you know."

"It's not fair. Now I can't see what your eyes are saying."

He wasn't at all in a hurry to take her hands off his eyes or to make her stand back. Her soft feminine scent enveloped him, and her warmth and charming softness was wrapping his soul with irresistible care. He, in fact, didn't need to see her eyes to know exactly what her body was saying: that she wanted him as much as he wanted her. He wished that she would lean close and lay her head on his chest and stay there the rest of the night.

And then, surprising herself and him, Katherine did just that.

Jack's didn't move at first. Katherine's hands slid down Jack's face and slowly down his chest, her fingertips for a moment brushing against the dark chest hair at the edge of his shirt. Her eyes met his with a tender honesty and surrender, and he thought he had never seen a woman whose eyes were so pure and revealing. Her hands slipped around his waist and finally pulled him to her as he brought his arms around and surrounded her in a warm embrace.

She lay her head on his chest, and she could hear his heart beating strongly and feel his breath calling her. She lifted her eyes again and looked into his. They shined just like hers. *He was right*, she thought, *the eyes can talk*. His were saying, *I want you*, and hers were saying, *I want you too*.

The moment lingered between them until Jack lifted Katherine into his arms. She was as light as one of the feathers that floated around them earlier that day when her pillow had burst. She closed her eyes and waited. His lips brushed softly against hers; he was so close that she could almost taste his kiss. His sweet breath was still ripe with the wine that they had shared. She counted his heartbeats as they pounded against her chest. Five and still no kiss. Six and still nothing. Nine and still he didn't move.

Jack watched her face for clues. Ten heartbeats had passed, and Katherine was ready to give up. He obviously didn't want her as much as she wanted him. Disappointment filled her heart, then right at the end of his eleventh heartbeat, she felt her lips conquered by his.

His conquest was firm and brisk; there was a sense of urgency as his lips pressed into hers. Her lips surrendered and opened up, allowing his wine-laced tongue to pass between them to caress hers Her tongue retreated at first then challenged his to a duel.

With her feet still held a few inches off the floor, she felt the space behind her moving. Perhaps it was his kiss that had the strength to move mountains that was carrying her or perhaps it was vertigo as her life's blood surged through her veins, to her head and back to her burning heart. She didn't care as long as his lips stayed on hers and their tongues danced together. She felt his grip ease, then she gasped as their kiss broke and she fell backwards onto her bed. Her arms around his waist brought Jack down with her. She opened her eyes to see the tiny white feathers somersaulting in the air before snowing down and covering them both.

Oh the weight of a man, she thought as his body moved above hers. She gasped, fearing that she had said it out loud. Not any man but a nice man, a funny man, an intelligent man, a sweet man, and yes, a very aroused man. She could feel his desire for her through the layers of clothing that separated their yearning bodies.

His manly heat smoldered beneath his clothes, and she grasped helplessly at the fabric of his shirt. He wanted her not because she was an attractive woman but because she was uniquely her. The girl who bumped into things, who couldn't brush her hair without tangling it, who was afraid of a chicken and had feathers stuck all over her. What he couldn't feel with his body, he felt with his soul. He could feel how much she wanted him, how much she needed him, and how much this moment meant to her.

Jack suddenly blew strongly into her face, and a feather that had stuck to her nose took flight. She giggled and, before her lips closed, they were caught again between his. She held him tightly in her arms, and she circled his leg with hers, then in a move that caught him off guard, she twisted her body and flipped him over onto the bed. Her delicate curves lay on top of him, feeling his desire beneath her. Their lips unlocked for him to hear her giggles once again as the feathers rose and fell in a gentle flurry.

She was in control right now, and she had everything that she had been wanting right here in front of her. She couldn't believe that this handsome and wonderful man was in her bed. Her finger traced circles over his cheekbone and along his jawline as she looked down at his beautiful face, almost as if to see if he was real. She kissed his forehead, his eyelids, the tip of his nose, once, twice, thrice. She kissed his right cheek then his left; she kissed his chin, enjoying the manly scuff of his unshaven cheek as she covered him with soft kisses that trailed onto his neck. She inhaled deeply the masculine scent of his skin and nibbled the sensitive skin of his neck.

They both gasped as their desires aligned between them. Katherine's eyes were two blue moons filled with light and charm as she gazed down at him then leaned in to kiss him again. Now that she had him, her lips couldn't bear to stay away from his skin. His hand on her back found her zipper and started pulling it down. She nibbled on his earlobe as the open gap in her dress revealed her back. She gasped when his bare hands caressed her sensitive skin, sending goosebumps chasing to every part of her body. Her lips moved from his earlobe to his neck to his cheek and clasped his lips as he unclasped her bra.

Her fingertips were nearly electrified as she touched his skin beneath his shirt as she opened it slowly one button at a time. She ran her fingers through the dark hair on his chest and didn't stop until his chest was bared to her. At the same time, his fingers were patrolling the edge of her panties, and her roaming hands quickly undid his belt and unbuttoned his jeans. She felt him tremble as she brushed lightly against his growing desire.

Just as she touched his zipper, he suddenly turned and rolled over on top of her, gently crushing her beneath his weight. She felt the full force of his longing, and she wanted all of it. She was ready to shed her last line of defense and surrender to him; the thin fabric of her dress was the only thing that separated her from the passion and love that she yearned so desperately for.

She drew in a quick, sharp breath as his warm, strong hand lowered her dress and cupped her bare breast. The lights flickered, and she gasped again, more out of fear than of desire. His arm around her held her tighter as her whole body stiffened each time the lights flickered. The lights wavered still again, and breathless, Katherine suddenly placed her hands on Jack's chest and pushed him away. She jumped away from him as if she had burned her skin on something too hot to handle.

He didn't resist but instead laid on the bed next to her, gasping for air. He didn't know what happened. His mind reeled. They were almost there, they were good, they were happy, and they both couldn't resist each other. Yet she pushed him away one second after she pulled him in. She turned him down the moment that she wanted him the most.

Jack closed his eyes and focused on slowing his heart rate down. His head throbbed as his elevated blood pressure began to decline. He had to think of something, anything, to calm his desire and get her out of his mind. He began to silently recite the only line that came to his head, repeating the mantra to slowly regain his composure.

The quick brown fox jumps over the lazy dog...The quick

brown fox jumps over the lazy dog... The quick brown fox jumps over the lazy dog...The quick brown fox jumps over the lazy dog.

"I have to go," Katherine suddenly announced.

Jack kept his eyes closed as he could feel the bed shift under him as she moved and stood up to leave. Her loosened dress almost fell to the floor, and her bra did drop with a whisper onto the artisan woven rug at her feet, but she didn't pause to pick it up. Instead she only pulled her dress up and reached back to zip it quickly. In her haste, the zipper stuck halfway. Jack opened his eyes and sat up, watching her looking around the room and struggling awkwardly with her zipper. Despite his anger and frustration at her, he was amused seeing her disoriented like that.

"I can't find my shoes," she said angrily and kept looking around.

She looked under the bed and beside the wardrobe. She looked on the dresser and behind the drapes. They were nowhere to be found; her shoes disappeared into thin air. She made another round and shed a few feathers and picked up a few more when she kneeled to look under the bed again.

She finally stood up and reluctantly looked at Jack. He grinned, and she wondered what he could find so funny in this situation, then he pointed to her feet. She looked down and found her shoes already on them. She had never taken them off.

I'm losing it, she thought, chastising her own lack of grace. I'm really losing it...Get it together, Katherine.

She spun around and charged towards the door, her long hair loose and streaming behind her. She yanked it open and stormed out, slamming it closed behind her. Jack waited for a few seconds then went and stood by the door and started counting.

Ten...nine...eight...seven...six...five...four...

He was interrupted at three with a knock on the door.

Katherine pushed through the door past him, leaving him

standing there in the aftermath of her tantrum.

"This is *my* room," Katherine snapped as she went straight to her bed, falling all onto it and burying her head under a pillow.

Jack was still upset, but he grinned as he stepped into the cool night air. The chill was welcome and refreshing and helped to tone down the heat in his cheeks and mellowed the rampage of lust in his body. He closed the door quietly behind him and inhaled long and deep then exhaled slowly, releasing his frustration along with his breath. He walked up to his room without looking back; he wanted this night to be over with. He had to shake this feeling, he had to erase this effect she had on him and put her out of his mind. He could only think of one thing to distract himself.

The quick brown fox jumps over the lazy dog.

***

The Koutsoyannopoulos Wine Museum in Santorini is unique in all of Greece. It documents the island's wine making history from the seventeenth century until present day. A thousand-foot long labyrinth buried in a cave twenty-five feet below ground. That's were Katherine was this morning, and it couldn't be more suited to her mood. She wished she could stay there for the rest of her life, unseen by the rest of the world, and, most of all, hidden away from Jack.

A few tourists were taking the tour with her. She pretended to be interested in the tools, vessels, and machinery that the winemakers used. She found the technical part a bit boring, but she was also impressed by the lifelike displays of figures doing the different tasks in the winery. She was particularly taken by a vignette of a man tending an antique wine press while a woman crushed the grapes with her bare feet. She almost leaned to kiss him if she hadn't been stopped by a very angry tour guide.

The best part for her was the final stop on the tour. The

wine tasting. Although she was already intoxicated from the lack of sleep, she gulped each and every glass that she was presented with before the wine expert could say a word about it. After four glasses, she bought a couple of bottles and left to go to the Minoan excavation site in Akrotiri at the southern tip of the island.

Akrotiri was a Minoan Bronze Age settlement destroyed in the Theran eruption about 1500 BC and buried in volcanic ash, which preserved the remains of frescoes, objects, and artworks. Akrotiri was the inspiration for Plato's story of the legendary island of Atlantis that sank into the ocean in a single day and night of misfortune.

There she sat in the shade of an ancient wall, took her shawl off, and placed it between the wall and a bottle of wine. She then stomped the bottle carefully until the cork came out. *Genius*, she thought to herself. She started drinking straight from the bottle, taking a couple long chugs and swallowing it.

She was half through the first bottle when she recognized one of the tourists visiting the site. He was Jack's German neighbor, and she was a bit surprised to see him awake and recovered from his night of drunken merrymaking.

"Hey Hans!" she called.

He recognized her and came closer.

"My name is Karl," he said with a heavy English accent.

"Hans, Karl, eins, zwei, drei, vier or even Rudolf or Guinevere," she replied. "What's the difference? Sit down, man. Have a drink."

"It's not even ten," Karl said but sat next to her anyways.

"You and your rules," Katherine said and handed him the bottle.

He grinned and took a swig.

"Too bad what happened to the Minoans," she said after taking back the wine bottle and swallowing another swig herself.

"But I tell you...they saw it coming. Now who lives at the edge of a huge active volcano and expects it to just sit there?"

Katherine waited for Karl's answer, instead he extended his hand to take the bottle, but she gave him a California handshake instead.

"You're weird," he said with a chuckle. "I like that."

"Hey, where did you leave your women?" Katherine suddenly remembered. "Careful Hans, I hope you didn't leave them at the hotel because your neighbor might steal them from you."

"They're on their way to Holland right now," Karl said. "So don't worry."

"Holland is the Netherlands, right?" she asked and Karl nodded. She wrinkled her nose thoughtfully then asked, "So who the hell are the Dutch?"

Karl started laughing.

"Who are they, Hans?" she asked urgently with a completely serious look on her face.

"I've seen that on TV...What's the name of that guy?" Karl asked as he tried to recall the name. "Seinfeld," Karl said, answering himself. "You're weird *and* funny."

"Nothing else, Hans?" Katherine asked seductively.

Karl didn't say anything; he just watched as Katherine leaned into him and kissed his lips. The bottle between them fell and spilled the remaining wine on the ancient excavated ruins. Katherine didn't care and neither did Karl, unable to resist a pretty girl's advances. He started kissing Katherine back, and their kiss quickly became deeper as she pulled him in closer.

"Hey!" a voice shouted. "What are you doing here? Look what you've done!"

Katherine unlocked her lips from Karl's and opened her eyes to see an elderly couple who had been strolling past and was now pointing at the wine spilled on the floor of the ruins. She was barely able to stand up but managed to pull herself to her feet. She looked at Karl who was still sitting and pointed her finger at him.

"He did it!" she slurred. "Hans did it."

She slumped back down onto the wall beside him, closed her eyes, and passed out on his shoulder. He supported her and shrugged apologetically at the couple who looked at them with disdain and walked away.

***

"Where am I?" Katherine asked, barely opening her eyes as she lifted her head a little then let it drop again.

She was groggy and disoriented, but she could see a light fixture hanging above her, similar to the ones found in an operating room. She frowned and wondered what had happened to her, and then she realized that she was reclined in a firm, padded chair. She thought for a moment and decided that it must be a dentist's chair.

What the hell I am doing in a dentist's office; she wondered and rubbed her eyes.

She looked around the darkened exam room and found she was alone, and the entire place was silent. She tried to get up, but her head throbbed and she got a little dizzy. She let herself collapse back into the chair again. The clock on the wall read 2:00 in bold digital numbers.

Is it two am or pm? she wondered.

Suddenly the door opened and someone turned on the lights, blinding her as she squinted and shielded her eyes.

"You're awake," a cheerful Maria said as she came into the office wearing a white lab coat.

"Maria?" Katherine asked in shock, failing to lift her head more than a few inches off the chair.

"Wait. Don't get up. I will bring the chair up."

"Where am I?"

"At the train station," Maria teased as Katherine smiled weakly.

Earlier in the day, Maria received a phone call. She recognized the number as Katherine's since they had exchanged numbers the night before, but there was a man on the line informing her that Katherine had passed out, drunk, in Akrotiri. Half an hour later, Katherine was lying in Maria's dental office, sleeping it off.

"I am sure you have patients," Katherine said after drinking the water and taking the aspirin Maria gave her. "So I'll just go."

She tried to get up again but failed miserably. She thought there must really be something potent in this Greek wine to hit her this hard. Every time it passed through her lips, she lost all control of herself.

"I was taking the day off. I only came in because I had an emergency at eight in the morning."

Katherine opened her eyes wide, remembering something.

"Was it a woman in her mid-thirties, wearing a white dress with black flowers all over it?"

"Exactly!" Maria replied. "Do you know her?"

"What did she tell you?"

"Nothing...that she fell and lost her front tooth."

"What else did she tell you?"

"Nothing. Why are you this worried?" Maria asked then paused a little and looked at Katherine suspiciously. "Is it because Jack brought her here?"

Katherine kept quiet. She shifted her eyes and stared at the wall in front of her. She looked worried and ashamed and sad all at the same time. Maria's woman's intuition allowed her to read all of that from one look. She softly laid her hand on Katherine's and squeezed it a little.

"She will be fine, by the way...I was able to save her tooth, but she needs to have some more work on it back home."

"She left?"

"That's what she told me she was going to do. Now tell me what happened?"

Katherine hesitated before confiding in Maria. She just met the girl and she was Jack's friend but still there was something in Maria that she trusted. She knew she could trust her not to tell him anything. It was, after all, part of the unspoken "girl code" that girls stick together, right?

She took a deep breath and began to recount all of the events that unfolded between her and Jack after they left Maria and Yiorgos, even the ones that she had hoped the alcohol would erase from her memory.

"So after he went back to his room, what did you do?"

"I cried for an hour and then some," Katherine confessed. She hung her head in shame. "The man didn't do anything wrong, yet I pushed him away."

"Maybe you weren't ready."

"Trust me...I was...every inch of me," Katherine continued as Maria blushed at her revelation. "But I remembered something, and it made me freeze."

Maria listened intently yet didn't want to push her. She sat quietly and waited for Katherine to speak.

"I am not ready to tell you what it is, not yet."

"I understand."

But Katherine was ready to tell Maria what happened after Jack left. She just stayed, lying on the bed in the same position, a pillow over her head and tears in her eyes. Memories of her past came rushing to her, and no matter how much she tried she couldn't shake it off.

At around three, she must have dozed off because she dreamed that she was flying over a volcano with a coffee cup in her hand. She dipped into the sea, filled the cup with water, and poured it over the volcano. She tried a thousand times, but the volcano was still spitting hot lava. Then she got close to the volcano and started falling in it, and before she fell completely inside, a strong masculine hand grabbed hers and lifted her up.

She woke up to the sound of roosters calling. *Damn those chickens,* she muttered, half asleep. She took a look outside, and dawn was just breaking, but it was still too dark. She lounged back on the bed, and as soon as she closed her eyes, she remembered Jack's weight over her as they sank into the bed together. She remembered how much she wanted him to stay there, and she remembered how much he wanted that too.

Katherine then thought that she did the right thing. It would have gone for days, weeks, and then what? She would leave like the Minoans left, their civilization destroyed just like her and Jack's hearts would be. She had to tell him her thoughts, she owed him an explanation, but how could she face him after what happened?

Katherine waited until sunrise and checked herself in the mirror. She brushed the small white feathers off her red dress and smoothed away the wrinkles in the fabric as well as she could. She fluffed her hair and hoped that he wouldn't notice the telltale puffiness and dark circles under her eyes.

I'm no chicken, she said, looking at her reflection in the mirror. She bolstered her courage and walked out of the door, through the courtyard, and up the stairs towards Jack's room.

She made sure this time that she got the right door. The German guy would be too busy and too naked to open his door. She hesitated for a few seconds, gathered her thoughts, rehearsed her piece, and knocked once.

It was more of laying her knuckle on the wooden door because she didn't even hear the knock. She took a deep breath and tried again. This time she heard it and heard Jack's voice call from inside, ordering her to wait a minute.

Please don't be shirtless; please don't be… she repeated in her mind as she waited with her eyes closed. She didn't want sexy morning Jack to appear, with his muscled abs and his bulging…

"*Nei?,*" a woman's voice came from the open door.

Katherine opened her eyes and saw a woman standing at the door. A beautiful woman wearing a white dress with a black floral print. At first she thought that she got the wrong door, but then she heard Jack's voice inside. Her legs told her to run, but she couldn't move until Jack came to the door and zipped up the woman's dress and gave her a kiss on the lips.

Jack took a glimpse at Katherine but didn't say a word to her, and he just bid the mystery woman goodbye. Katherine didn't say anything because she felt that her heart was about to stop. *He was just another man looking for sex,* her mind was telling her. How could she be so foolish to think that she felt something between them, a connection and feelings of an emotional nature? He was, after all, just a guy who didn't want to spend the night alone, and he seemed to have filled the vacancy quite quickly.

Katherine's legs finally obeyed her, and in a flash, she started running down the stairs. The woman was walking down slowly in front of her, and Katherine pushed past her and continued on her way, then behind her, she heard the woman cry out as she tumbled on the stone steps.

Katherine looked back and saw Jack running down the stairs towards the woman who warmed his bed last night. *His damsel in distress,* Katherine thought sarcastically then felt a pang of guilt. The woman was cursing a thousand curses a second in Greek while Jack was kneeling beside her, inspecting her injuries. She could see that the woman was bleeding from her fall on the stone step, so she turned to go back to help.

Jack raised his hand to halt her from coming any closer as he comforted the crying woman.

"You've done enough, Katherine," he snapped angrily. "I think you should go."

She reluctantly walked away then stood by her door as Jack carried the woman back to his room. She escaped into her room, threw herself on her bed, and started to weep as a cloud of little white feathers settled around her.

"This will help," Maria said softly. "Take it. It's the perfect drug."

Katherine looked suspiciously at Maria and hesitated a little. Then she smiled and took the extra-large bar of chocolate she was offering her. Maria was the most understanding dentist she had ever met.

Beware of Greeks Bearing Gifts

Katherine was holding a gift box of chocolate in her hands as she knocked on Doctor Vasilis's door. She had expected a housekeeper to answer the door, judging from the size of the house and his status in the community, so she was surprised when his thirty-two year old daughter opened the door. Katherine recognized her as the woman from the port who was leaning into Jack's personal space and handling him like a piece of choice meat. She began to cheerfully introduce herself but was hastily interrupted

"Yes, my father is expecting you," the woman said rather coldly. "I'm Cassandra, Doctor Vasilis's daughter...you can come in."

Cassandra's English was even better than her father's; her British accent was very pronounced and even her looks were not as typically Greek as the other islanders. The woman was courteous but not too welcoming. Katherine related that to being jealous about seeing her with Jack, but it could be anything really. She tried to excuse it as the woman merely having a bad day.

They traveled through the house, and although it was typical of the architectural designs of the island, it was also very modernly decorated. The marriage between the old and the new, the traditional and the high tech, was very tastefully done. It was also much bigger than the houses surrounding it, and its location high on the cliff side made it seem much more palatial.

Katherine followed Cassandra into the opulent living room. The room was beautifully illuminated by the late afternoon sun; ahead of them was a wide glass door leading to the terrace. It truly looked like something from an interior design magazine, not someone's actual home. Cassandra noticed the fascination on Katherine's face and smiled, nodding in approval.

"He's sitting next to the pool," Cassandra announced. "It's a beautiful day…Try not to ruin it by knocking anyone's teeth out." Her tone was casual as if she rehearsed that line a hundred times before.

Katherine gasped and couldn't believe what she just heard. Cassandra's words pinched her right in the butt like a bee sting. She stopped walking and hesitated between going out to see Doctor Vasilis and leaving this obviously very small island all together. She didn't even bother to ask Cassandra how she knew about the incident that only she and Jack had witnessed. Jack didn't have a big mouth - *although he had very delicious lips-* but he couldn't have told her.

"Just for the record, it was an accident," Katherine began defensively. "And the woman stumbled on the steps and hit the railing."

"I believe you," Cassandra said and leaned a little towards Katherine, as if she held a secret. "Between you and me, she deserved it."

Katherine was now sure that Cassandra was not only jealous of her but of Aphroditi too. She was obviously into Jack, and Katherine was the enemy of her rival, but that didn't make them friends, obviously. In this case, Cassandra's venom was not one she wanted to be subjected to, so she decided, at most, to be cordial *frenemies*.

"Coming?"

Katherine dismissed her hesitation and followed Cassandra

out onto the terrace. It was small by Western standards but big enough to have a small infinity pool and seating for ten or twelve people around it with luxurious pillows and chaises. The views were stunning as the bright turquoise pool shimmered and sparkled, and the design of the pool was such that the water overflowed its rim, leaving little differentiation between the edge of the water and the crystalline sea beyond it below. Anyone in the pool would have the feeling of being at the edge of a high waterfall that flows into the caldera.

"Papa!" Cassandra called, softly alerting Vasilis from his reading.

"Ah! Welcome," he said as he stood up to greet her. He was warm and courteous, unlike his daughter's frigid reception. "I'm glad to finally officially meet you."

"I'm conscious this time," Katherine blurted out, saying the first thing that came to her mind.

"You look marvelous. Please have a seat."

"These are for you," Katherine said, handing him the elegantly-wrapped box of chocolates.

"Thank you," he said graciously. "It's a nice treat to have on Easter Sunday." He placed the box on the small side table next to the book he had been reading.

"Papa is very strict during Lent," Cassandra said. "He doesn't eat anything but fruits and vegetables."

Katherine wasn't sure if that was a criticism of her gift or merely an observation.

"And coffee," he said warmly. "How do you like yours?"

The contrast between Doctor Vasilis and his daughter was very apparent. He was kind and welcoming, while Cassandra, although well educated, seemed to be lacking in the social graces. She put on a good show, but her words were biting and rude.

"I'm surprised that you don't know," Katherine answered and

then regretted her sarcasm when Vasilis lifted his eyebrow curiously. "*Vari glykos*, thank you."

She thought she saw Cassandra roll her eyes as she left to make the coffee and wondered if she pronounced it wrong. She and Vasilis sat in the shade, basking in the magnificent view, the expanse of brilliant blue sea trapped in a lagoon between majestic rocks. It looked like a one vast dark blue eye that never blinks.

"I hope you didn't feel any headaches after your incident," Vasilis said, breaking the silence.

"No, not at all. I can't thank you enough for what you did, and Theodora told me that you refused to be paid."

Katherine noticed that Vasilis's face lit up the moment he heard Theodora's name. It was so obvious that those two were very much in love. A love that forty years couldn't wipe out of his memory.

"She did most of the work anyways. I just supervised."

Cassandra came out with the coffee and sat down on a chair next to her dad after serving them. She had a glass of mineral water with a twist of lemon for herself. She eyed Katherine critically from head to toe, leaving Katherine feeling suddenly very underdressed and wishing she had worn something more elegant than her simple pink knee-length dress.

"I love your sandals," Cassandra said.

"Thank you," Katherine said to her nemesis. "They're from Milan. I bought them last summer."

"You travel a lot?" Vasilis asked.

"I've been traveling non-stop for the last two and half years."

"Really?" Cassandra said with obvious curiosity.

"And I know from experience that this place is the most beautiful that I have ever been to," she said with all honesty. "I really wonder who would ever want to leave this place, other than the Minoans of course."

Both Vasilis and Cassandra laughed.

"You have a beautiful house, by the way."

"Thank you. My grandfather built it after he returned from Brazil," he said. "Obviously, some do leave and come back."

"What did he do in Brazil?"

"This is going to be a long story," Cassandra said with a sigh before her dad could answer. "It's time for my swim if you don't mind."

"Not at all," Katherine said as Cassandra forced a smile and went inside.

Katherine waited for Doctor Vasilis to start telling the story of his grandfather. His worries that she wouldn't be interested dissipated from the look on her face. She was very interested to know. In fact, it was the best part of her journey to so many countries. She had gathered thousands of stories that could fill volumes, and one day she planned to write a book about them.

"My grandfather's name was Christos, and since he was a little boy, he used to sit with his great uncle who would tell him stories about the days he spent in San Francisco during the Gold Rush."

"Really!?" Katherine exclaimed. "I'm from San Francisco."

"Then you are going to love this," Vasilis said excitedly.

Cassandra emerged wearing a white bikini, which Katherine thought was too immodest to wear in front of her father. It was very revealing, and although Katherine was happy with her own body, Cassandra's curves and tanned skin made her envious. She had a very sexy body, and the push-up effect of her bikini made her small breasts look much bigger and rounder than they really were.

She removed the sarong from around her waist and dipped her toe in the water before plunging in. She made a splash, but all the water went the other way, and Katherine and Vasilis were only caught by a few drops. Although the pool was only thirty feet long,

Cassandra had memorized its dimensions by heart and lapped it back and forth a dozen times before taking a short break.

Meanwhile, Katherine listened intently as Doctor Vasilis continued telling the story of Christos:

His grandfather, impressed with the stories of the great riches that California had to offer and being stuck on an island that had a limited future, sneaked out one night. Taking all his savings from working with his dad in the butcher shop, he hitched a boat ride to Athens. It was his first visit there, and since he didn't know anyone, he had to sleep on the docks of Piraeus.

A week after that, he found a ship sailing to São Paulo, and they told him that from there, he could take a ride to San Francisco. He was twelve at the time and didn't know that the two cities were thousands of miles apart or that they were not even in the same hemisphere. Since he didn't even have the full fare, he was expected to work in the ship's galley. For the next twenty days, he spent over twelve hours a day in a hot and humid room below deck, peeling and boiling potatoes.

Once he arrived, Christos didn't understand why he left Greece in the summer and reached Brazil in the winter. It was only twenty days at sea, and he already leaped two seasons ahead; this must be the land of magic. He asked around on ways to reach San Francisco. Those who didn't understand what he was saying shooed him off, and those who did laughed him off.

It took him one week to realize that he was tricked and that he had to find work fast or he would starve to death. Odd jobs were plenty and easy to find, and the pay was minimal, but he needed just enough to get him to San Francisco, where his real journey would begin. One day while going to work in a butcher shop, almost one month after he arrived, he saw a guy dismissing a street vendor after he discovered he was stealing from him. He approached the guy and found out that he had over twenty street vendors working for him.

He offered to take the job that the dismissed employee left vacant, and he was convincing enough to get it.

The first few days were very hard, and he didn't sell much. He even received a blow from his employer as a warning for his bad performance. In fear of losing his job, he combed the streets for customers. One afternoon, he was walking next to a school in an affluent neighborhood, and it was dismissal time. The very well-dressed students started coming out of the main gate. At first, a couple of them saw him and came and bought from him. Then some others saw him too, and he made a few more sales. Fifteen minutes later, he was out of stock.

His employer didn't believe that he sold all his supply of candies in one day and that Christos was demanding to carry double the goods the second day, but seeing the money and knowing that Christos' only source of income was his job, he had to believe him and take a chance on him. The second day the same thing happened. The school boys also demanded some other products, more expensive ones, which he gladly provided.

In one week, Christos made more than other vendors made in a month. Everybody dismissed his sudden success as an anomaly that would soon wither away. A month later, however, Christos was earning three times more than the highest earner among his colleagues, and for him, the San Francisco dream was within reach sooner rather than later.

Rumors started flying around between his colleagues that he had found a golden spot, and some wanted to snatch it from him. The next day, five of them came to his spot and waited for him. He saw them and kept walking towards the school gate with confidence. The boys thought that Christos was an easy bait and soon his butt would be kicked and the earnings would be all theirs.

What they didn't know was that Christos had one more trick up his sleeve, one he learned while working at the butcher shop back home. A few people at the shop used to get special treatment and the best meat without ever paying for it. He learned that they were people with authority, people who could come handy in a time of need.

Across the street from the school, there was a police station, and all of its members received free treats daily from Christos. In no time, he became their favorite friend and he knew that his smart generosity would come handy one day. And that day had finally arrived.

As soon as Christos assumed his position, he was swarmed by five boys. They knocked off his table and started abusing him. One even punched him in the nose, and blood started running down his chin. A police officer saw what happened, and in no time, the five boys, who had run once they heard a police whistle, were chased and brought to the station. Christos didn't want any harm done to them, but he made them promise to leave him alone, and they gladly complied. They too were indebted to him now because he had saved them from receiving any discipline for their bullying.

In the following years, Christos learned from where to get his supplies, and he started his own business. His old rivals became his employees, which he spread out in strategic places all around town. Soon, all people with influence owed him favors, and that helped him expand unrivaled. With his business savvy and entrepreneurial spirit, he eventually branched out into many businesses, and before long, he owned shops and restaurants and coffee plantations. At the age of twenty-four, only twelve years after he landed in Brazil, he became one of the wealthiest men in São Paulo.

All of this didn't mean anything, though, in a country where he was impressing people he didn't know, people who after all these years remained strangers to him. In his mind, he was a candle lit in broad daylight. The only place where he would be really recognized was if he went back to Santorini, where everyone would be impressed by his success. They would all say, *"Look what Christos, the son of Nikos, did and how many gold coins he brought with him."*

He also had his eye on Kassiopi, a girl one year younger than him, who lived in his old neighborhood and to whom he promised a gold ring when he returned from San Francisco. He remembered her face as if he had left yesterday; her brown eyes, sweet smile, and tiny nose were still fresh in his mind. He had to go back and hope that she was still waiting for him.

Despite the raging First World War all over Europe, in 1915, at the age of twenty-five, Christos decided to go back to Greece, go back to Santorini, back to Kassiopi. He sold his business despite an offer from the city mayor himself to become his partner. He also offered Christos his gorgeous young daughter for marriage. Christos declined and headed back home on the first available ship, after converting all of his fortune into gold coins and one gold ring. This time, he boarded as a first class passenger with almost five tons of cargo stowed beneath, and the most valuable item was kept in the captain's safe.

"The things that we do for love," Katherine said dreamily, interrupting Vasilis' story.

"Love is the most powerful of emotions," Vasilis said. "Be it for another person or for power or one's country,"

"My princess," Cassandra called from the far side of the pool. "And her favorite handsome teacher."

She swam to the edge nearest to the glass door leading to the terrace as her daughter Eleni walked through it, followed closely by Jack. Eleni bent and kissed her mother. Jack offered his hand to Cassandra, who then pulled herself up out of the pool then stood gorgeous and dripping wet in her small bikini. She offered her lips to him, but he kissed her cheek instead. Eleni noticed that they had company and recognized Katherine from the other day when she went and played with Alexandros.

Jack saw Katherine from the second he stepped onto the terrace, but he pretended that he didn't see her until he helped Cassandra out of the pool and helped her dry herself with a towel. Vasilis introduced his granddaughter to Katherine and reintroduced Jack too, although he knew that she already knew him well.

Cassandra confiscated Jack's attention as he sat next to her, leaving a few seats between them and her father and Katherine. Eleni went and brought a couple of glasses of orange juice for her and her teacher then sat next to her grandfather. Katherine couldn't help but notice the half-naked Cassandra was going out of her way in seducing Jack, who seemed now to be very interested in her.

"Aren't you feeling cold, sweetheart?" Vasilis asked his daughter, hinting about his daughter's immodesty in front of guests.

"I'm fine, Papa. Don't worry about me. I'm not a little girl anymore."

Of course you're not a little girl, Katherine seethed silently. Your hard nipples are pointing at Jack, ready to pop out. She had to bite her tongue to keep her thoughts from spewing out.

"You will always be my little girl," Vasilis said with a smile and went back to his story with Katherine attentively listening and at the same time eavesdropping on Jack and Cassandra.

Half of the cargo Christos brought with him from Brazil were supplies for a desperately-needed medical center on the island where he had a hero's welcome. At last, he was able to consider what he had achieved as a success, only because he saw it through the eyes of his own people. There was still one thing that he needed to do. He needed to show one woman what he had accomplished in his time away from Santorini and now how much he could offer her.

He looked for Kassiopi's face, but she was nowhere to be found. He then asked his mother about her, but she didn't answer him. He then went out into the village to find her or someone who could tell him where she was. He saw Kassiopi's father who at first tried to avoid him but with some coercion, he finally told him with tears in his eyes that his daughter had tragically died the previous week. Complications during childbirth had claimed the life of his beloved, leaving behind her first child, an orphan son who never knew his father either because he had been killed in the war two months before the child was born.

"Oh!" Katherine cried out and almost shed a tear.

Vasilis stopped talking, and Jack and Cassandra watched Katherine's reaction. They had all obviously heard the story a thousand times because even Eleni took it lightly. A small tear rolled down Katherine's face and was immediately wiped out with her hand.

"Tell us a story to cheer us up, Papa. You made the woman cry," Cassandra teased.

"It's ok. I want to know what happens next," Katherine insisted.

"In the meantime, I will bring you something to cheer us all up," Cassandra announced as she stood up. "Eleni come help me." She paraded her body in front of Jack, making her intentions obvious, then leaned towards him and whispered in his ear, "Don't go anywhere."

Katherine was shocked that she would act this way in front of her young daughter and even more so that she would do so in front of her father.

The fiery sun was blazing on the horizon, ready to be extinguished by the Aegean Sea, and Doctor Vasilis paused to point it out to Katherine. She had been too intrigued by his story to notice the beauty of the scene unfolding just over the edge of the infinity pool. She was mesmerized and caught herself holding her breath at its stunning allure.

"No matter how many times we watch the sunset, it is always fascinating," Katherine said a moment later.

"And no two sunsets are ever the same," Vasilis commented.

Jack admired Katherine's face and saw the beauty, the passion, and the sweetness. He knew that we are always our true selves when we are the most vulnerable, and Katherine's emotional response to the story of Christos and her reaction to the raw beauty of the sunset were very attractive to him. Her face reflected the feeling felt by Christos almost ninety years ago, but now all he could see was how her cheeks blushed when she noticed him staring at her.

"Please continue," Katherine said to Vasilis, putting her hand lightly over his.

Christos realized that he did all that he did for nothing. He spent years away from his family and from the love of his life to come back and find that she was gone. He wished that he had stayed and enjoyed his time with Kassiopi, but despite his pain and chagrins, Christos decided to go into action.

He went and asked to see Kassiopi's baby, whose grandparents were taking care of him. He had been named Dimitris, and Christos was immediately charmed by him. He was a happy and handsome little man, and he offered to take care of the boy as his own and even suggested adopting him. His grandparents were reluctant at first, but they finally accepted once he promised to let them raise him and never take him from them.

"He built this house and a few others, opened businesses, was a great asset to the community," Vasilis continued. "And became a wonderful father to my dad."

"So Dimitris was your father," Katherine said, and Vasilis nodded. "And Christos your grandfather but you are not blood related."

Vasilis smiled and nodded again.

"Love is much thicker than blood," he said with a sigh.

"Did you ever know him?" Katherine asked. "I mean your grandfather."

"Of course. He lived to be ninety-one, and I used to spend

hours with him telling me stories about his past."

"Did he get married?"

"Yes, in his forties, he did get married, and he had a son...my uncle...who immigrated to Australia in the Sixties. He used to come here every couple of years, but after his dad died, he stopped, but we are still in touch."

"I'm curious about something," Katherine said. "Did he ever make it to San Francisco?"

"I knew you would ask me that," Vasilis said with a warm smile. "He never had the chance, but when I used to ask him, 'Grandpa, how much do you love me?' He would answer, 'I love you from here to San Francisco'."

"How sweet," Katherine said with a soft smile. Jack noticed when her beautiful, tiny dimples emerged at the corner of her sweet lips and tears welled in her eyes.

The sentimental moment was interrupted when they heard Cassandra and Eleni returning, singing *Happy Birthday*. They turned to see Cassandra carrying a birthday cake with lit candles on it, and Eleni was holding two presents. Jack stood and gasped at the surprise birthday party. He watched them as they approached the table, smiling and shaking his head in disbelief at the scene.

"It was my idea," Eleni bragged as she gave Jack his gifts. He bent down to hug her and gave her a quick kiss on the forehead.

"I helped her," Cassandra said and stood like a little girl waiting for her hug and kiss after she placed the cake in the middle of the table.

She had changed into a short blue dress with golden leaves on it. It was a very flattering design and style, and Katherine felt a pang of jealousy once again. She didn't wait too long for Jack to hug her, as she quickly leaned into him with her eye on Katherine's reaction. She kissed Jack's neck and caressed the small of his back as Katherine looked on.

"Happy birthday," Katherine said, staying seated. "If I had known, I would have brought you a gift."

"Thank you," Jack replied. "No one other than Eleni knows my birthday, and she tricked me into telling her when it was."

"*Haroumena Genethlia, Hronia Polla*, happy birthday and many happy returns, my dear friend," Vasilis said with a smile.

"Thank you, Doctor. I don't know what to say really."

"Don't say anything now," Cassandra purred as she pawed all over Jack. "Just make a wish and blow the candles."

"And open the presents," Eleni cheered.

After Jack blew out the candles and everyone had a slice of cake, except Doctor Vasilis, who had a small plate of fruits instead, Jack opened the presents. The first one from Eleni was a figurine of Nike, goddess of victory and Jack's favorite Greek goddess. Cassandra's gift was an obviously very expensive Omega watch.

"So that you never forget your happy moments," Cassandra said as she kissed Jack again and leaned into him.

Katherine felt nearly nauseated at Cassandra's display, and she felt the need to leave. She couldn't bear to see another woman all over the man she was kissing last night, and he wasn't protesting too much. She hadn't recovered from this morning's double disaster with Aphroditi's tooth incident and the Minoan shameful wine spill. She had to leave before a third disaster occurred, because in her mind, she was pushing Cassandra into the pool.

She excused herself and said was getting tired. She made the excuse that the intrigue of Christo's story had exhausted her, which wasn't far from the truth. The goodbyes and more birthday wishes took almost five minutes. Although she and Cassandra were both interested in Jack, Katherine remained kind and courteous while Cassandra's forced politeness was transparent.

Doctor Vasilis showed her out, and she thanked him again for his care for her after her fall and his great hospitality today. She told him how delighted she was that he shared his grandfather's story with her and that she would never forget it. She was a little bit distracted though, before stepping out of the main door, by the loud laughter coming from around the pool with Cassandra leading the choir.

As soon as the door locked behind her, she texted Maria.
I need a drink.

We're Even

Aphroditi had finally calmed her anger after a disastrous day and unsatisfying night. She wasn't sure if she was angry because of Jack or his attractive neighbor or at herself. It was almost eight, only two hours until the next ferry, a ferry that she missed once this morning and was determined not to miss this evening. She was desperately in need of a glass of wine or at least a beer, but she was advised by her dentist not to consume alcoholic beverages as long as she was taking pain killers.

She had to admit that Maria did a great job on her and saved her tooth after that crazy woman that looked like she slept the night in a hen house knocked her over. She was also hungry, and all her attempts at eating anything but yogurt failed. To make matters worse, she was extremely frustrated because she didn't get what she came for last night, and that completed the perfect storm she was in the middle of.

The owner of the coffee shop she was sitting in suggested a cold drink and offered it on the house to her when he saw how much she was in pain. Although she wasn't short of money, his gesture made her smile for the first time since yesterday. *Finally something is going well*, she thought.

She was contemplating recent events when a guy came to talk to her. She was usually receptive to flirtations, even if she didn't have the intention to act on it, but this time she went out of her way to decline even a casual conversation. The mood was not right, and her tooth and lips hurt every time she thought about opening her mouth.

Aphroditi's phone rang, and it was her husband calling. Spiro worked as a first officer on a merchant ship. He was supposed to be home for the next three months, but a couple of days after he arrived, he received a call informing him that his replacement got sick and had to be medevaced off the ship. They needed him for a few weeks until they could find a proper replacement.

Spiro was ten years older than she, and he never planned on getting married. He was already married to the sea, as he used to always say. Aphroditi didn't want to get married either; she had a carefree, free-loving spirit and she couldn't see herself tied down to one man or one place for very long. She came from a family of small olive oil producers on Crete, and after everyone was gone, she had been left to take care of the business. She met Spiro five years earlier, and they became good friends and occasional lovers. The relationship suited him as he only spent half his time with her and the other half with a ship somewhere in his beloved sea. The relationship suited her because she kept her freedom and independence.

They got married one year after they met, honeymooned for a couple of weeks, then Spiro sailed away and she went back to work. Aphroditi wasn't a fool, and she knew from the beginning that Spiro had other "lady friends" in every port he visited. Although she felt lonely with him away for long periods of time, the inconvenience of taking a local lover outweighed the benefits. Jack had been her only occasional bed buddy.

Aphroditi stepped outside to take the call. The ship was about to sail from the port of Piraeus, and she wished him a safe trip.

As she turned around to go back inside the coffee shop, she bumped into someone who was rushing to get out. She lifted her eyes up, and there she was, her arch-nemesis, the American woman from Hell.

"You!?" Aphroditi shouted and moved back with rage building inside her.

"I was just leaving...I swear!" Katherine stuttered. "I came in a second ago and I saw you outside, and I decided to leave...Please don't hurt me."

"I'm going to kill you!" Aphroditi shouted, her eyes narrowing, no longer the refreshed and carefree vision of beauty that had appeared at Jack's door the night before.

"But you look great," Katherine said, taking one step back.

Aphroditi took a step forward, holding back her anger but ready to pounce.

"I didn't know that you were there, I swear," Katherine pleaded. "I am so sorry. I will do anything you want...please!"

Just then, Maria came out of the door and stepped between the two women. She put both hands on Aphroditi's arms and talked to her in Greek, calming her down. It seemed to work since Aphroditi stepped back and her rage subsided.

"Now let's all sit down and have a talk like adults," Maria said.

***

King Priam and Queen Hecuba of Troy had nineteen children. The most famous of them were Hector, Paris, and, of course, the prophetic Cassandra who predicted the fall of Troy. She had red curly hair, blue eyes, and milky white skin. She was described as being the second most beautiful woman in the world after Helen of Troy.

Mythical Cassandra was intelligent, desirable, and sweet. Her charm and elegance was enough to bring Apollo, the God of light and the sun, healing, music, truth, and prophecy, to his knees. One night as she was sleeping in his temple, he commanded the snakes to lick her ears, giving her the gift to hear the future. Despite that, Cassandra refused Apollo's seductions until he cursed her so that her predictions would not be believed, leaving her in constant pain and frustration.

Modern day Cassandra was named after her. The moment she was born and her father saw her red hair, he said, "Cassandra". She was the spitting image of her mother Abigail, the English woman who Doctor Vasilis married despite his parents' objections. The young couple thought that a child would change their old-fashioned Greek minds, but although it softened their stance, it certainly didn't change it.

Cassandra was two years old when her parents brought her to Santorini. Like her mythical figure, she also predicted the future. She predicted that her mother would leave, and she did as soon as Cassandra turned twelve. Island life wasn't Abigail's cup of tea after all. Although she frequently visited her daughter and Cassandra spent a few years in private school in London a half hour away from her, she felt that her daughter was closer to her dad than to her.

Years passed, and Cassandra made another prediction; this time it was her own divorce. People on the island said that their family was cursed; she said that her ex-husband simply didn't like her cooking. She never planned on getting remarried until she set her sights on Jack. She had a couple of boyfriends in the last few years, but they never moved beyond bed-buddy stage.

Jack was different than the others. He was smart and mysterious. He was intelligent, well educated, and cultured but without arrogance and had a quick wit and down-to-earth sense of humor. He was handsome and soft, yet rough and manly; he was equally at home at formal events in a tailored suit or in jeans while helping out a neighbor or friend in need. He was a magnificent lover, tender and giving, focusing on his partner's pleasure more than his own. He could be so close and intimate then suddenly inexplicably detached and distant. He could make a woman wait for him for ages, frustrate her with his aloofness, yet she still wanted him more and more. Cassandra's fire was raging, and this evening she was determined to make it consume both of them.

Soon after sunset, Eleni was picked up by her father, who she was supposed to spend the rest of the week with. It wasn't a minute too soon for Cassandra, who had made other plans for the evening. Her father had a plane to catch for a conference he was attending in Thessaloniki, and he insisted on driving himself to the airport at seven so as to not inconvenience anyone, leaving his daughter and Jack alone sitting by the pool.

"Eleni adores you," Cassandra said after turning on the romantic soft lights in and around the pool and sitting on the chair next to Jack.

"She's a lovely girl. I know all this was her idea."

"I helped," Cassandra said, putting her hand over Jack's and smiling an innocent little girl's smile.

"Last month she tricked me into telling her when my birthday is."

"I know it's on Thursday, but since she will be away for the next couple of weeks, we decided to make it today, despite my dad's objections to do it after Easter."

"It was a wonderful surprise."

"Now that we are alone…" Cassandra said, pausing for anticipation with Jack lifting his eyebrow, curious what was coming next. "White or red?"

Jack only replied with a quiet pleasurable "Mmmmmmm" that drove Cassandra wild inside. She batted her eyelashes at him and smiled softly.

"The wine, love...white or red?"

"Red would be great."

"What did you think? I was making you guess the color of my underwear?" Cassandra joked. "Naughty boy," she said provocatively as she stood up and went inside.

Jack leaned back enjoying the cool breeze that was picking up the scents from around him, the sea and the jasmine. He closed his eyes as his other senses picked up the sounds and smells. It was barely a minute when he felt lips softly kissing his. He knew it was Cassandra, for her perfume engulfed him. She lifted her head, and he opened his eyes as she came from behind and sat next to him. She smiled as she poured wine into his glass and hers.

"*Hronia Polla*," she said as she lifted her glass.

"*Efharisto*," Jack replied, lifting his own glass.

"What did you wish for, Jack?"

"I wished that I will live on this island a thousand years," he answered after hesitating for a moment.

"Lovely. I will have you here next to me," Cassandra said enthusiastically and spit three times in her cleavage. "Give me," she added, reaching for Jack's hand.

Jack looked puzzled since she was already caressing his other hand.

"Your hand. I want to read your palm."

Jack reluctantly gave her his palm. He never believed in superstitions, but it's hard not to when you live in the Greek Islands, where superstitions preside. Whenever you are afraid of jinxing yourself, you spit on yourself. Whenever your shoes land soles up, you straighten them and say *skordia*, which literally means garlic. If you have an unwanted guest, sprinkle salt behind them and they will go away. *Filahta,* or talismans, are always found pinned on the clothes of infants. Avoid also, at any cost, saying that a child is beautiful; nothing will bring more joy to his mother than spitting in its face three times.

Fortunetelling is also practiced on daily basis through coffee cups or palm reading. Women all over Greece are predicting the future of thousands of people at any given time. Most readings are just an innocent pastime, but some are taken very seriously, and some women are known to accurately predict the future.

"You know I don't believe in those things," Jack said, resisting a little.

"When a beautiful woman asks you to give her your hand, you do it."

Jack immediately complied; Cassandra was both beautiful and sexy. He wasn't afraid of that, but she was also good at fortunetelling, according to her reputation. That worried him and made him reluctant to give a beautiful woman his hand.

Cassandra took his hand in hers. She caressed it, running her fingers all over it. It was both ticklish and exciting for Jack. She looked him deep in the eyes, lifted his palm to her lips, and kissed his open hand. Her lips lingered for almost a minute. The softness of her lips sent shivers down Jack's spine and warmth all over his skin.

Jack lowered his eyes, unlinking them from hers as she gently lowered his hands onto her lap. Her finger traced a line across the middle of his hand. This time, her eyes indicated that she was reading something.

"You only see the good things in people," she said. "You can't restrain your emotions when you love someone."

Jack didn't respond to that, and Cassandra never lifted her eyes off his palm to probe his reaction to what she just told him. She just kept tracing lines across his palm. If she had looked at him, she would have read that he was more interested in her caresses than the palm reading itself.

"You have a vivid imagination," she continued. "That shouldn't come as a surprise." They both smiled, and she continued.

"But you're reluctant at first. You only take chances if it involves someone else," Cassandra said and pursed her lips. "For a woman maybe."

She waited for an answer that didn't come, but she knew that she was right, and she didn't need his approval. Cassandra noticed that Jack wasn't taking her too seriously, so she decided to give him something to think about by going deeper into his past.

"One night, you slept a millionaire, and you woke up broke," she said.

His eyes narrowed and he tilted his head slightly, suddenly interested in what she was reading.

"Someone broke her promise to you," she then said.

"What do you mean?"

"She said she would come back, and she never did."

Jack's face whitened as if it was instantly deprived of blood. His palm started to get cold, despite Cassandra's warm hands. He suddenly had the urge to take his hand back and flee, but his hand wouldn't move. Cassandra sensed his anxiety, but she was determined to go through with this.

"Your life changed in a blink of an eye. Fire and smoke prevented you from seeing someone." She paused then added, "A woman, a very beautiful woman."

She wanted to continue, but suddenly she was feeling so emotional. Jack started to pull his hand away from hers, but at the last moment, she gripped it and held it tightly in her hands. She closed her eyes and took a deep breath then started reading again.

"I see a key on the bottom of the sea," she said. "It looks like an old house key. It looks rusty as if it's been there for two or three years." She cocked her head and then said, "I see a woman in a blue dress. She dips her hand and picks up the key and walks away over the sea."

Cassandra suddenly looked puzzled. She looked at Jack and

then looked at his palm again. She saw something, but obviously she didn't want to tell him. He saw the reluctance on her face. He wanted her to say it no matter what it was but waited anxiously.

Jack felt a tear drop fall onto his palm, then another one then another, all coming from Cassandra's teary eyes. He dropped to his knees in front of her and put his hands on her arms and then brushed his fingertips over her tear-streaked cheeks. She closed her eyes and leaned forward then kissed his forehead.

"What it is it?" he asked gently.

She didn't reply. Tears kept pouring out of her eyes and onto Jack's hands. She swallowed hard and shook her head left and right as if she wanted to shake off the vision she saw. Jack urged her to tell him what she saw.

"What is it? What did you see?"

"Something terrible is going to happen?" she said with her voice breaking, filled with emotion.

"Is someone going to die?"

"Worse."

"What could be worse?"

"You're leaving Santorini for good."

***

At the end of the hour-long heart-to-heart session, Katherine and Aphroditi were sitting together, laughing like old friends. At least that's what any outsider would think. They were laughing because Aphroditi just told Katherine and Maria what really happened the previous night with Jack. It took her a little while to tell the story since she was too afraid to talk at her usual pace in fear of biting her lip because it was still numb from the anesthetics.

As soon as she knew that Spiro was called for work early, she started planning a surprise visit to Jack. She delegated a couple of tasks at work, put on her sexiest lingerie and sweetest dress, and off she went to Santorini, taking the airplane this time. She arrived at around ten and went straight to Jack's room.

Jack wasn't there, but his door was unlocked. She went in made herself at home and lounged in his bed. Then she heard some loud noises coming from the courtyard. She immediately took her dress and lingerie off, draping her bra on the chair where Jack did his writing and laid her panties in an obvious way on his table. That would be the first thing he would see as soon as he came in.

Then she started hearing German songs and girls giggling and laughing. She was sure that the man's voice was not Jack's, and she was certain when moments later that man barged into Jack's room as she was adjusting the covers over her breasts. He took a good look at her lying seductively on the bed, the girls flanking him, then apologized, realizing it wasn't his room and went out again. The thick walls prevented most of the erotic sounds that the three's company soon emitted from the adjacent room.

Less than fifteen minutes later after she arranged herself seductively again on the bed, a terribly agitated Jack suddenly came through the door. He was mumbling to himself as he walked in. She smiled and pushed her chest out, tossing her hair over her shoulder, but he didn't notice her; it was as if she was invisible. He sat in his chair and switched the table light on. Still mumbling, he started to frantically type on his Smith-Corona. A couple of minutes later, he froze and turned around, his eyes wide as if he saw a ghost.

Aphroditi was lying in his bed, her perfect naked skin glowing in the light emitted from the small lamp on the night stand, giving her an ethereal quality. The shades, shadows, and umbra that her lounging silhouette cast all over the room were enough to bring any man crawling to her. For a man who had already explored her succulent topography, Jack should have dived in a heartbeat. Instead he froze, his pulse raced and then subsided.

Aphroditi immediately got the message; his reluctance killed her. She immediately rose from the bed and slinked across the room towards him, her hips swaying from side to side. She bent and kissed his lips and laid her hands softly on his face. She looked into his eyes and saw his pain.

"Who did this to you?" she whispered softly to him.

She had undressed him and led him to the bed, where she held him tenderly as he slept until dawn. She couldn't sleep herself because she knew that they were over. He barely said anything, but she read it in his eyes. There was definitely another woman, a woman that meant more to him than any of the intimate pleasures they had once shared.

Aphroditi was heartbroken, but she always knew that this day would come. What she always imagined was that it would be over between them when Jack eventually moved on and left the island. She never thought that he would still be near yet unattainable. Her consolation was that they had the best of times when they were together, and she hoped that he would remember her fondly.

At dawn, once Jack woke up, he couldn't find enough words to apologize. He vaguely explained to Aphroditi his reasons, and all she did was put her index finger to his lips to shush him. She didn't want to know any details that might taint the memory of their times together. She wanted to keep it as simple as the day they first met.

"As if the insult you caused wasn't enough, you came in the morning to inflict the injury," she said, pointing at Katherine.

"I'm so sorry. I really am. You can't imagine how much."

"I would love to stay and chat, but now I have to run," Aphroditi said. "Thank you, Maria, for saving my tooth." Aphroditi stood up and looked to her right, smiling at the coffee shop owner.

"So we're good then?" Katherine said, still seated, wanting to be sure that there were no hard feelings left between them.

Aphroditi took a deep and long stare at her. She slowly lifted the half-empty water glass off the table and threw the water in Katherine's face. Katherine wiped it off slowly as if she expected it.

"Now we're good."

"One more thing," Katherine called after Aphroditi as she turned to leave. "What was Jack typing?"

"Something crazy...about a brown fox and a lazy dog," she said with a shrug. "A*ndio*," she called over her shoulder as she strutted away.

A Thousand Islands

Jack appreciated the distraction the students offered him at the local school of Fira. They were just about to finish their last lesson of the day. He had completely forgotten that he had accepted that invitation a couple of weeks ago and was only reminded by a call from the English school teacher a little bit before eight that morning.

Her idea was to make him an all-day celebrity guest on the four lessons she gave on that day to different grades at the school. In this way, he could interact with students from different levels. It was more fun than he expected, and the interactions were lively and very interesting.

"Remember… reading is the key to writing," he said at the end of the session.

A couple of students stayed after class to discuss a few things with Jack. Both of them borrowed his books once they knew he was visiting, and apparently they knew more details than he could remember. After satisfying their curiosity, he and Elena, their teacher, went out for lunch. Later, a couple more teachers joined them, and for some mysterious reason, they were both females.

He thought of the irony of sitting with three females after losing three females yesterday. First Katherine, then Aphroditi, then

Cassandra, who after the palm reading started crying and confessed her love to him. She begged him not to leave and told him that she fell in love with him the second they met on a very windy day back in 2001.

He was about to come back from the airport after dropping someone off. He slipped and fell outside the airport; her dad, who was waiting for her, took care of the scratch his knee sustained from the fall and offered him a ride back to Fira. She got into her dad's car, only to find a handsome American stranger sitting with Eleni in the back seat, telling her a story.

That day, her father invited Jack to his home, and they all sat and talked. Then Cassandra, who desperately wanted to get closer to Jack, offered to read his palm. He was excited because he had never had his fortune read. That day she told him something that he would never forget. *You just kissed someone goodbye for the last time.*

A week later her, prophecy came true. He never saw that person again, and their final kiss at the airport was their last. That's why he was so reluctant to give Cassandra his hand again. He even tried to avoid prolonged conversations with her to avoid any more heartbreaking prophecies.

Telling him that he was going to leave and never come back was incredibly farfetched since he never left the island since he arrived in the summer of 2001. Her emotional breakdown and tears, however, made him worry. Not because she loved him, he knew that a long time ago, but because she was certain that what she saw was true.

"We were betting on who could read your thoughts right now," Elena said, waking Jack from his distant thoughts.

"I was thinking about how lucky I am to be sitting with three beautiful ladies."

Jack was saved by his wit, and all three women walked out winners. They stayed there for another thirty minutes before they said their goodbyes. As Elena drove him back to his place, he could have sworn that he caught a glimpse of Katherine in a taxi as it passed them on the narrow street. Her image not only haunted his thoughts; he seemed to see her everywhere.

He wanted to check on Nikos and Theodora, but he thought he'd better go straight to his room since it was very close to siesta time and he would see them in the evening. He passed through the courtyard, fighting his urge to knock on Katherine's door. He resisted well enough to reach his room, where he almost tripped on a package left on his doorstep.

It was half the size of a shoebox, lightweight, and gift wrapped with silver paper. Jack brought it in with him, looked for a card, and didn't find one. He shook it, and something barely moved inside. He was curious but still not ready to open it, so he tossed it on his bed and went and took a shower.

When he came back, the box was still on his bed waiting to be unwrapped. This time he took the call and peeled off the shiny paper cover to unveil a hinged wooden box; judging from the quality, he thought it must be rosewood. Jack opened it, and there he found a small card with elegant, feminine handwriting on it.

Happy Birthday. I thought this would suit you, Mr. Steele.
Katherine
P. S. Peace, until we meet again.

The box contained a very elegantly crafted wooden pipe. Jack smiled when he remembered what Katherine told him earlier, that she thought all writers should smoke pipes. He then took it out of the box and held it up. He brought it to his lips and thought of it as a peace offering, the same way that the Native Americans offered the Pilgrims their pipe when sealing a peace treaty.

Jack placed the pipe carefully on his writing table next to his vintage typewriter. They looked great together and made that portion of the room look like a scene from the 1950's. Katherine understood him despite all that happened yesterday with her and because of her. Suddenly he had the urge to see her, to talk to her, even to kiss her. Jack ran out the door and down the stairs, and ten seconds later, he was knocking on Katherine's door.

"I just wanted…" he began as the door opened. He suddenly stopped and took a step back from the door. *"You're not Katherine,"* he said in shock.

"No I'm not," the woman replied. "Can I help you with something?"

"What are you doing in Katherine's room?"

"I don't know any Katherine," she said, becoming irritated by his interruption. "This is my room. It might have been Katherine's room at some point, but this is a hotel. People come and leave all the time," she replied dryly. "Anything else?"

"No," he said, just before she closed the door.

Jack took a couple of steps back, turned around, and walked slowly through the courtyard until he reached the edge. He looked out across the endless sapphire sea in front of him. He knew that he had spent so much time in one place that he forgot that it was a hotel. He had made a home of what was supposed to be a temporary residence.

He watched a ship leave the port, its silvery waves shimmering behind it, and assumed that Katherine was on it. He suddenly felt a soul-crushing emptiness inside him, unlike anything else he had ever felt in his life, and tears filled his eyes. She left without him having a chance to say goodbye. He wanted to look into her eyes one more time. The only problem was that he didn't know what he wanted to say. *Stay?*

"Jack, did you eat?" Theodora called him from the other side of the courtyard. "Come. Have a bite with us. You look pale."

Jack complied, and although he knew that he wasn't pale and that he had eaten less than an hour ago, he wanted to ask Nikos and

Theodora about Katherine. They sat in the reception area and converted the front desk into a very nice dining table. It took him half an hour and a dozen forced bites of food to ask about her.

"So when did Katherine leave?" he asked abruptly.

"You miss her already?" Theodora asked, almost seeming to have expected the question.

"Oh no, but she left me a birthday gift, and I didn't have the chance to thank her."

"Hmmmmm…" Theodora hummed with a slight grin on her face.

"Seriously."

"She left this morning."

Jack took the information and waited for more. Theodora was too economical in her answers, while he on the other hand wanted to know if Katherine asked about him before she left. He needed to know if she said where she was going, and most importantly, was she coming back?

Theodora, on the other hand, had played this game so many times for so many years. All she had to do was wait, and eventually Jack would reveal his true feelings and ask the right questions. Seeing that everybody had eaten their last bite, she gathered a couple of plates and stood up to take them to the kitchen. Jack started to help her, when she told him to sit down and relax.

"Where did Katherine go?" he asked Nikos the moment Theodora left the room.

"She didn't say," Nikos began, and Jack's heart sank into the deepest murky depths of the caldera. "But I think she is still in Greece. Maybe taking a tour around the islands."

"Really?"

He tried to contain his interest and excitement, but his reaction gave it away.

"She asked many questions about the islands, so I think she

went there."

"There are islands other than Santorini you know," Theodora said, entering the room. "More than a thousand. You should visit them some time."

"But they don't have your delicious cooking on them. That's why I stay."

"I will stop feeding you then."

"You want me away so bad?"

"I want you happy. That's all," Theodora said and pinched Jack's cheek.

He dreaded asking her if she thought that he wasn't happy, but he preferred not to. Jack was instead relieved that Katherine was most probably still close by. It wasn't that he was going to follow her around, but it was possible that she would make another stop in Santorini before she left on her next adventure. That thought alone made a look of heartbreaking sadness wash over Jack's face. He looked defeated as he slumped in his chair. His sadness could not be more apparent to Theodora.

"Where is your suit for the wedding? You didn't get it yet?" She asked changing the subject to a lighter tone.

"It will be here in a few days."

"I need time to do the alterations."

"Everything will be perfect for Yiorgos's wedding. Don't worry."

"Get yourself a bride, and we will make it a double wedding."

"That's my cue," Jack said quickly and stood to leave. "I will see you in the evening." In the blink of an eye, he left the room, dodging Theodora's suggestion.

***

The last thing Katherine expected to see from the window of the small, single-propeller airplane was a windmill. Not just one, but probably a dozen dotting the hills overlooking *Chora,* commonly known as Mykonos, like the island that it is built upon. The windmills are to Mykonos what the caldera is to Santorini, the most noticeable attraction of the island.

The flight took less than 20 minutes aboard the small propeller airplane, but the hop was filled with a magnificent Birdseye view of a thousand islands dotting the Aegean Sea. The only words that Katherine thought of in her mind to describe the view were a*bsolutely stunning.* She even imagined herself floating in the air, stepping on each island, and leaping towards the next, like a magical game of hopscotch. It was almost if she was passing through a dream of shining azure in between white rocks and sandy beaches.

The Island of the Winds, as Mykonos was nicknamed, is also the party island of the Aegean Sea. It is frequented by the upscale crowd who are seeking a stylish nightlife, transforming the otherwise sleepy island into an ongoing party. Although summer is the peak tourist time, young college students may hop for a weekend on any given month for some fun times, relaxation, and, of course, one might be lucky enough to find a spontaneous lover or two.

Katherine deplaned on an island that was bustling with college students on Spring Break. She stepped into the middle of an ongoing party of stamina and raging hormones. She realized that when she got a few whistles from a bunch of guys who were barely above the drinking age, when a gust of wind betrayed her and lifted her light blue dress way above her waistline.

It was a little bit chilly and not very beach friendly, but once Katherine arrived at her hotel on the southern part of the island, she was surprised by the number of sunbathers basking in the sun. Most of them were from northern parts of Europe, who at this time of the year, are still surrounded by white snow and ice and gloomy skies rather than sun, sea, and white sand. Katherine immediately changed into her bikini, and off she went to join the young and adventurous.

***

Anyone looking from the outside into Jack's room would have sworn that he was meditating. Sitting up straight but motionless in front of his desk, his eyes closed and his breathing effortless keeping his heartbeats low. His hands placed palms down on the old scratched wood top desk, close but not touching his vintage black typewriter. Rays from the low afternoon sun were beaming in on him, putting him in the spotlight like a stage actor who was about to perform.

Rare were the days where he sat at his writing desk this late in the day. He was a morning person, he only sat there to write, and he only wrote in the morning. Today was an exception, and he was sitting there having a strong urge to spill some emotions in the only way he knew how, by putting ink on paper.

Jack opened his eyes and quickly removed the paper with the hundred quick brown foxes and lazy dogs dotting it from top to bottom. He placed it squarely and precisely on one corner of his desk, grabbed a blank white page, dropped it down effortlessly on the feed roll behind the platen roller, then twirled the platen knob clockwise, a ritual he had to complete over and over again every time he filled a page. It was a great contrast from typing into a word processor on his iMac; a typewriter makes the process itself more romantic, nostalgic, and crafty.

He smiled as he remembered when he bought a typewriter and read a fifty year old manual on how to use it, and he still got it wrong after the first seven hours of serious attempts. There were so many things to do, from putting a new ink ribbon in to setting the page gauge, the page margins, the line spacing, and figuring out how to go to the next line, but at dawn his inked-stained fingers managed to type his first sentence: *The quick brown fox jumps over the lazy dog.*

Since then, the sound of the keys hitting the paper and the rhythm of his fingers dancing over the keys then pausing to return the carriage after the small bell dinged cheerfully at the end of each line became part of his process. He couldn't complete any work now without his trusty sidekick.

This evening, he started the last chapter of the newest book in his Anny series. It was the fifth one and the fourth written on this same desk using this same typewriter. A little bit after midnight, the last page was completed. He put it face down and flipped the whole stack up and started reading the whole book, finishing four hours later. He then closed his eyes and went into a deep sleep; it was like climbing a mountain and finally reaching the peak.

***

While Jack managed to distract himself with writing and reading all night long, Katherine was out partying with a very young and vigorous Spring Break crowd of college students. The girls were all dancing on the beach in their bikinis despite the cold, flaunting their taut, lean bodies for the guys who braved the chill shirtless, showing off their muscular physiques. The chilly wind was heated by a large bonfire in the middle of the improvised sand patch dance floor of the notorious south beach of Mykonos.

For once, she was the most hit on girl in a party, and it soothed her damaged and aching heart to be desired this way. She figured that her more mature figure with fuller breasts and the lush curves of her hips were the reasons why every young man wanted to dance with her; some of the younger girls shot her dirty looks as she was taking some of the attention away from them. The guys were outnumbered to the count of "two girls for every boy", yet it seemed that nearly every one of them only had eyes for Katherine. The real estate surrounding her became so sought after that guys literally fought for it. They competed on who wanted to fetch her a drink or get her a folding chair to sit on once she felt tired from the dancing.

She was the sexy teacher that every school boy dreamed of. She was too old to be their colleague, yet too young to be their mother. Katherine was that hot French teacher who you saw at a party being herself outside the comfort zone of the classroom where she has control.

"You look like Xena," a young guy who was barely over eighteen said as he kneeled beside her and handed her a bottle of beer.

Katherine paused for a second and started laughing. She expected everything but that. Kids these days would say anything to a woman to impress her, but that was a first. She was flattered and humored, and she had to stop laughing before she broke that poor boy's heart.

"The warrior princess," she said and smiled. "Well, thanks...I guess. Does that then make you Hercules?" She fluttered her eyelashes softly to flatter the boy.

Katherine didn't know if it was the glow fire that was raging ten feet away or all the activities under the sun earlier in the day, but that young man's face flushed crimson when she spoke. She also noticed that a couple of his friends were watching him talk to her, as if they were waiting for something. He still didn't answer her question; he was quiet like someone who had rehearsed his line and didn't expect the answer. She bet that he didn't even expect her to even talk to him so he hadn't prepared his next line in the scenario.

"Come," she said as she stood and moved her chair to the side. She sat on the sand and pat the patch next to her. "Sit down next to me. My name is Katherine. What's yours?"

"Brian," he said as he sat down, in shock that she had invited him and afraid to sit too close. He even jumped a little when his arm brushed against hers.

"Hi Brian," she said, tipping her beer bottle towards him and waiting for him to clink his into it.

She smiled, looking at his handsome features. He had short blond hair and probably green eyes, but she couldn't tell from the dim light. He had a sweet face, still holding the features of youth before turning into full manly type and losing forever its innocence. Brian was tall, but his body wasn't Herculean; his physique was lean with the mildly-toned muscles of a boy on the verge of manhood.

"What brings you here?" Katherine asked.

"We're on Spring Break, so we decided to come here. Cool place, isn't it?"

She had thought of many words to describe the Greek Islands in her time there, but "cool" had not been one of them.

"It is," she said in agreement. "And who are you with?"

"Friends from college."

He pointed to the guy and the girl who were sitting across from them on the other side of the sandy area. They had been watching intently but now went back to playing a game of Spin the Bottle on the sand with some of the others.

"So you all decided to come here?"

"It was Keg's idea," he said, pointing to one of the taller and more muscular guys. "His name is Kevin, but we call him Keg cause he can lift a full keg of beer over his head."

"Cool," Katherine said with a light laugh, delighted with the brainless conversation she hadn't had for years. "So what's the dare?"

"What?" Brian said with a shock.

"Come on, Brian. I saw your friends staring, waiting for you to do something," she said as she tipped her head towards him. "Come clean, and we'll see what we can do about it."

"They dared me to kiss you," he shyly confessed and looked down at the sand.

Katherine laughed as Brian turned all red. He was too shy for a college boy, rare these days, and totally sweet, she thought. She loved the fact that she was the object of desire for young specimens. It wasn't a big deal, but she was glad to know that she was still in the game, literally in the game.

Brian was going to get that kiss tonight. She wouldn't embarrass him in front of his friends, but she wanted to linger on a little more, make the experience more enjoyable for both of them. It wasn't something sexual for her but more of a fun thing to do.

"I bet you that Keg came up with the idea."

"How did you know?"

"He's the type," she said taking a glimpse of Keg who was sitting next to a red haired girl with his hand caressing her bare back.

"But the Xena thing was all my idea."

"Was a good line. You got me."

Brian was confused and wasn't sure if Katherine was telling the truth or was just teasing. She could see that his self-confidence wasn't his best of qualities. Then she saw anger and sadness mixed together as he gazed through the flames of the bonfire at Keg caressing the back of the red haired girl. Every time he did that, she removed his hand and glimpsed at Brian.

"What's her name?"

"Who?" he asked, looking back at Katherine.

"The girl who's sitting next to Keg. Is she his girlfriend?"

"She's not." he said defensively, as if the word "girlfriend" pierced right through his heart. "She's Jessica. She goes to college with us."

"And you like her."

"I don't."

"Yes, you do, and she likes you too. I can see it from the way she looks at you, and just so you know, she removed Keg's hand many times off her back, and if you don't do something about it and do it soon, she will keep it there next time."

Katherine's words, although sincere, were too harsh for Brian to bear and were not what he wanted to hear right now. He was, in fact, in love with Jessica, his school friend and later his college friend. They had known each other for years, and they studied together since they were in middle school. He couldn't remember a day that he wasn't in love with her, but he never had the courage to tell her.

The blunt truth coming from a woman he just met was too much for him. He didn't know how obvious his fondness for Jessica was and how pathetic it made him look. He stood up and walked away without saying a word, dusting off the sand off his swim shorts as he went. Brian didn't look behind him; he went straight back across the sand and sat with his friends.

Katherine watched as they all laughed at him for failing to complete the dare. She knew that she played a part in that, although it wasn't her intention. She felt sad for him and had the urge to make it right. The bottle was spun again, and some guy kissed a girl sitting opposite of him.

"Do you want to come sit with us?" a guy's voice called from a short distance behind Katherine.

She looked around and saw that the people who were on the dance floor earlier were now sitting under the almost full moon. They were older than Brian and his friends, and they were obviously couples. From their accent, Katherine guessed that they might be French or Belgian.

"Yes sure, but there is something I have to do first."

Katherine stood up and walked towards Brian. She made sure to sway her hips seductively as she moved closer, and the circle of friends turned to watch her approach. She came to a stop next to Brian, directly facing Jessica and Keg, who both were staring at her.

"There is something I forgot to give you," she said softly, looking down at Brian.

Brian stood up after hesitating a little and almost lost his balance if it hadn't been for Katherine's supporting hands grabbing him from both sides. He stood up facing her, his height towering over hers. She smiled at him, and he blushed again as she slipped her hand behind his neck and gently pulled his head down to her.

Standing on her tip toes, their lips met in the middle, amidst staring eyes from Jessica and Keg, their other friends, the group sitting far away, and everybody within eyesight. Brian's kiss was shy and shallow. Katherine could press it on, but she didn't want to force it. She settled down, and their lips separated.

"Now kiss me like you mean it," Katherine said looking Brian straight in the eyes.

This time, he didn't hesitate; he crushed into her as she lifted herself up. She parted her lips for him, and he kissed her for real. He kissed her like he would kiss Jessica if she let him. Jessica was dumbstruck, and her mouth dropped open, watching Brian kiss that beautiful and sexy woman right in front of her eyes, making her flush with jealousy.

"That's how Hercules would kiss Xena," Katherine said after what seemed to be almost a minute of heavy kissing that almost got to her.

She turned and walked away towards the group who invited her to sit with them. She smiled with triumph when she heard the cheers of almost everyone on the beach. Katherine kissed a boy into a man tonight. *Beat that Xena.*

***

Katherine managed to get a few hours of sleep before she woke up the next morning, and off she went to the island of Delos with the three French couples who she met the previous night. They graduated from college last year, and they decided to take a year off before starting work. *You got to love those Europeans.*

Santorini

They were all from around Toulouse, a city in the south of France. After a short trip from there towards the coast, you would find the best nudist beaches in all of Europe. The French were not too conscious about their bodies, and naturalism was part of the lives of many, at least during the many long vacations that they took, a fact that Katherine came to realize once the three couples decided to skinny dip into the sea and invited her to join them.

After a short hesitation and seeing Laura, Maxime, Chloé, Julien, Pauline and Sébastien shed their swimwear and run through the sand and into the water, Katherine did the same and followed, *au naturel*. Nude beaches are available in the San Francisco Bay area, but Katherine never went in fear that someone she knew and didn't want to bare it all in front of would see her there. Here on Mykonos, the only witness who knew her well was the silver moon.

Katherine walked slowly through the sand, the cold breeze swirling around her naked body; it felt so refreshing after all of the stress and the chain of events that occurred on Santorini. The moon light shined off her tanned skin and reflected off its surface back into the eyes of the night. She walked like a Goddess into the arms of Poseidon, the great God of the sea, offering her body to him as he beckoned her like a waiting lover. The white foam felt like a thousand tiny fishes nibbling on her toes, and the waves splashed over her legs before the sea hugged her waist, like a favorite mermaid. All Katherine could think about was Jack emerging from within the folds of the waves and carrying her away.

Something Old, Something New, Something Borrowed, Something Blue

"Nikos! Theodora!" Jack yelled from outside the reception door.

He opened it and entered. The room was empty, but he could hear sounds of giggles coming from the other room. There was someone in Theodora's seamstress haven. Jack didn't hear words, only the joyful laughter of women and ooh's and ahs. He called Theodora's name one more time and decided to venture in.

What he saw next shocked his senses, rendering him speechless. His sudden entrance into the room nearly knocked the woman in the white silk wedding gown off balance from the pedestal upon which she was perched. He couldn't believe his eyes as he looked at this vision of beauty and elegance, so irresistibly white, sparkling, and glowing. The woman was none other than Katherine, who he thought that he would never see again. He felt frozen in time when he laid his eyes on her.

Jack was looking suave and debonair in his brand new suit and came to show it to Theodora to check if it needed any further alterations. Yiorgos and Maria's wedding was tomorrow, and Jack didn't want to leave anything to chance since he was the best man, and all eyes would be on him for the hour-long service. Yet now after ten days without her and realizing his true feelings for her, he stood looking at Katherine trying on Maria's wedding dress.

"There must be a cat here somewhere who ate both your tongues," Theodora mocked when neither of them said a word for over a minute.

They both started to speak together and then stopped.

"You came back," Jack finally said.

"I promised Maria to attend her wedding," Katherine explained. "I came to try the dress Theodora made me."

Jack looked up and down at the wedding dress with confusion.

"Not this one. Mine is the blue one," Katherine said, pointing to a dress on a hanger. "Then she insisted that I try Maria's dress."

"Oh look at you! You look amazing!" Maria called cheerfully from behind Jack as she came into the room, adding "*Ftou, ftou, ftou*".

Maria entered carrying a bag and placed it on the table then kissed Theodora and kissed and hugged Katherine. She commented again on how beautiful she looked in the dress.

"Not so fast, handsome," Maria said as Jack tried to slip out.

"I thought I'd give you some space. I can come later."

"Come here," Maria said, taking his hand and dragging him until he was standing next to Katherine.

"What are you doing?" Katherine protested.

"You look wonderful together," Maria said, stepping back to admire them. "I am pronouncing you man and wife!"

Theodora laughed and said, "But we will have seven years of bad luck. He already saw the blushing bride in the wedding dress."

"Blushing, huh?" Maria teased, winking at Katherine who pinched her lips together.

Both girls were hiding a secret from Theodora and Jack. Only three days ago, Maria traveled to Athens and met Katherine for a bachelorette party across the city. They went bar-hopping on a flirtatious escapade, where they ended up in a female strip club since they couldn't find one with male dancers. There were no pictures to commemorate the event, but the girls had a blast, a big contrast from Katherine's ten-day cultural tour across Greece.

Katherine arrived earlier that morning, and Theodora caught her before she went to her room. She whisked her away to her sewing room to try on the blue dress she made for her. When she was satisfied with the final fitting and the hem, she urged her to try on the wedding gown. Of course she had to since she was dealing with a relentless woman who wouldn't take no for an answer and because she also secretly wanted to see herself as a bride, something she thought she truly had no chance of seeing again in her lifetime.

"I need to take a picture," Maria announced, still admiring the view of Jack and Katherine standing side by side as bride and groom.

Katherine blushed some more; it all seemed too real for her to be standing with Jack as his bride. Jack was dumbstruck by the entire scene, and he felt his heart was about to stop. The camera flash woke him up as Maria came through with her suggestion and took a couple of pictures of them posing together.

"Now go and let us finish," Theodora said, dismissing him, and the game was over.

Before going out, he took one more look at Katherine in the wedding dress. Her eyes met his, and for a moment, they both wished that it was all for real. Bumping his head into the door while turning helped snap him out of his trance. He went straight to his room, took off his suit, changed into shorts and t-shirt, and went for a run. A long run down the winding steps, down to the caldera, and as far as his legs would carry him, until he gripped his side in pain and gasped for air.

***

Maria was helped into the wedding dress by both Theodora and Katherine. Some alterations were needed since Katherine had fuller breasts, and in a minute, the real bride fit perfectly into her wedding dress. Theodora's eyes were full of tears as she watched her son's bride all in white in front of her.

"I have never worn or touched something that soft," Katherine said describing the dress. "It was as if being immersed in molten chocolate."

"It was a parachute," Maria and Theodora said at the same time.

"It doesn't seem *that* big," Katherine said, trying to explain that the skirt of the gown wasn't too full as Maria thought. "Just wait until—"

"No!" Theodora protested to a confused Katherine. "It really was a parachute."

Katherine had come to love the interesting stories about everything there in Greece. It seemed like the Greeks had every aspect of their lives immersed in history. She realized that on her recent tour of the islands and the mainland. History in Greece, however, is not only collective; it is also individualized and everyone has his own grand historical event.

It was in the month of May 1941, after most of Greece had fallen into the hands of Nazi Germany, except for the island of Crete, which was facing the largest airborne attack ever launched before and since then. Theodora's grandfather and two other men were fishing in the deep waters surrounding Santorini when they noticed something floating in the water less than a hundred yards south of their location.

Earlier in the day, they had seen many German bombers and fighters heading south, and they feared that they might have dropped sea mines. However, the object didn't look threatening, but they all decided to approach it with caution. The closer they came, the more human like the shape became. Once they were a few feet away, they realized that it was a pilot or a paratrooper with the parachute still attached to him.

They lifted him up to their boat, still breathing but unconscious. The insignia on his clothes was clearly non-German, which made the rescue team happy and at ease. It was humanitarian to rescue your enemy, but it made it more humanly acceptable to rescue your allies. They gathered his parachute and put it on the boat too and headed back to Santorini.

He woke up a couple of minutes later when one of the men poured fresh water over his face. He was startled at first and feared that he might have been captured by German troops, but then he relaxed once he realized that he was among Greeks. None of them spoke English, and he couldn't speak a word in Greek either, but they understood well enough to give him water and some bread that they had with them on their fishing boat.

It was a blessing that they arrived after dark at the Island, and they were able to take him to Michalis's house, Theodora's grandfather, without anyone seeing them. Michalis's wife was frightened at first about keeping a soldier at her house and feared the retaliation of the Germans if they knew he was there. She then calmed down and ordered Michalis to get rid of the pilot's clothes by burning them. He also tried to get rid of his parachute, but once his wife Eirene touched it, she realized that it was made of pure silk. She washed it gently in fresh water to remove the smell of the sea from it then carefully dried it and kept it under her bed for safe keeping.

Flight Lieutenant Sam Pope was already serving in the Royal Air Force of New Zealand when his country declared war on Germany. Being a citizen of a British Commonwealth country, the words of his Prime Minister at that time, Michael Joseph Savage, were common sense: *"It is with gratitude in the past, and with confidence in the future, that we range ourselves without fear beside Britain. Where she goes, we go! Where she stands, we stand!"*

He was part of the Expeditionary Force that was helping the Greek troops in the defense of Greece. He was first deployed on the mainland, and when the mainland fell, his squadron flew to the Island of Crete to provide air support to the garrison on that island. The last thing he remembered was that he was locked in a dogfight about five miles south of Santorini before he got shot down. It must have been the tides that made him drift north closer to the island.

The couple and their three teenage children welcomed Sam as part of the family, but his presence didn't stay a secret for long. Almost a month later, Italian troops came and took him. It was a real blessing that Santorini fell under the Italian occupational force rather than their ruthless German allies or Michalis and his family would have suffered dearly. No one ever knew what happened to Sam until one day in 1953 almost twelve years after his rescue, when a man, a woman, and an eight year old girl appeared on Michalis's doorstep.

"I was the one who opened the door for them," Theodora said to Katherine, whose eyes filled with tears. "I was eight at the time, and my mother took me to my grandfather's house to help Grandma in making Christmas pastries."

"Oh!" Katherine cried. "Thank God he wasn't dead!"

"No," Theodora said and placed her hand over Katherine's reassuringly. "He was taken as a prisoner of war and was freed and sent back to New Zealand once the Germans retreated." She then looked at Maria who had tears in her eyes too. "Why are you crying? You heard this story a million times."

"Happy endings always make me cry," Maria said, wiping her tears.

"Then leave all the crying for tomorrow after the wedding," Theodora laughed.

Sam and his family spent Christmas and New Year with his

Greek friends, and that gave Eirene time to make his daughter a dress. He couldn't believe that the dress his daughter was wearing was once the parachute that brought him down safely into the sea.

"Then I got jealous because Grandma didn't make me a dress too," Theodora said. "So she promised me to make my wedding dress from the parachute silk."

"Amazing story," Katherine said.

"After my wedding, I'm giving it to you," Maria said to Katherine.

"I don't think I will ever get married, so don't waste it on me."

"Yes, you did, and I have the picture as a proof," Maria said, referring to the picture she took earlier of Katherine and Jack.

"I think I will go unpack now and leave you two to finish up," Katherine said, standing up and avoiding the subject.

"It's lunch time. You should eat first," Theodora said, grabbing Katherine's hand and preventing her from walking out.

***

The weather was lovely for a traditional Santorini wedding. It was breezy but not windy, sunny but not hot, and the nights were cool but not cold. Through the week long preparation, so many rituals were observed.

Tomorrow morning, before the wedding and after the morning Mass, the priest, Jack, Theodora, Nikos and Maria's parents would go to a vineyard carrying a carafe full of wine. There and on the sounds of live, traditional music played local musicians, the best man will pour the wine on a vine tree. The priest will choose two vine sprouts with many buds, which symbolize the many children that the union of the couple would bring to this world. The priest will then cut them then weave the vine sprouts into two wreaths, being careful not to break them, which would bring bad luck, according to local beliefs.

Then, the party will drink the wine left in the carafe, and the priest will smash it on a tree stump in the vineyard. After performing this ritual, they will return to the bride's house, where the wedding guests will be waiting for them. Young girls will take the vine sprout wreaths and begin to decorate them, covering the wreaths with cotton woven with golden threads, and finally they will tie white and colored ribbons to them.

The wreaths are part of the wedding ceremony, and as soon as their decoration is completed, the guests will leave the house and go to the church. Only the dressmaker will stay at the house to help the bride put on her wedding dress and to sew on it a small piece of paper with the names of all unmarried girls in the village written on it.

On the eve of the wedding, the bridegroom brings a chest filled with his clothes to the bride's house as the nuptial bed is made. Yiorgos felt so nervous, although he knew that he would be accompanied by his best man who was participating in this tradition for the first time, coached for a whole week by Nikos. The presence of members of his and Maria's family made him even more nervous. It would be a big party, and everyone would be having fun, but he felt like he would be scrutinized the entire time as if he was under a microscope.

"Have you ever felt that you want to just sleep and wake up the next day when everything has gone back to normal?" Yiorgos asked once he sat alone with Jack on the balcony of his house an hour before sunset.

"This is your new normal, my friend," Jack replied and then realized that his words were more alarming than comforting. "I didn't mean it that way."

"I know what you meant," Yiorgos said then hesitated then abruptly asked, "Do you think I'm ready for this?"

Jack wasn't surprised at all by Yiorgos' question. He expected it to come earlier in the week than the eve of his wedding. The problem was that he wasn't sure how to answer it without tainting his friend's decision with his own experience. Instead, he let Yiorgos talk and say what was on his mind. All he had to do was to listen attentively, nod occasionally, and make a very concerned face, just like a psychologist.

"I love Maria so much, I never loved anyone more than I love her, and I have no doubt that she loves me too," Yiorgos said then looked at Jack who nodded with concern. "But the question is will we stay the same as husband and wife?"

It was strange for Jack to hear these words coming from Yiorgos. His love for Maria was indisputable and genuine, but what he didn't like were the social pressures. Marriage in Greece was a social act, a carefully choreographed dance perfected over the years.

"Tossing children on a wedding bed?" Yiorgos asked rhetorically.

He was talking about the traditions that take place the night before a wedding after the groom takes his clothes to his bride's house since the tradition in Greece is for the wife to provide the house. All the groom has to do is to bring his clothes and remember to step in with his right leg first when he comes in through the door.

One of the traditions was the *krevati*, or making of the bed. The two families, relatives, friends, and pretty much most of Santorini and a few curious tourists gather together in the bride's house. After they all eat and drink, two young "virgin" girls make up the double bed, and the first to get a pillow case on will be the first of the two to get married. Then all the people present throw money on the bed, including gold coins to make the marriage prosperous. After the bed has been showered with money, a young male child is tossed on the bed, in hope that the first child from the union of the couple will also be a boy.

Yiorgos went on and on about the traditions and the rituals he had to go through all week long and how much more he had to embarrass himself before the wedding was over. The only problem was that traditions would continue even after the wedding.

All the time Jack was thinking, if Yiorgos can't handle it now, how is he going to handle it then?

"I can read your thoughts you know," Yiorgos said looking at Jack. "You are thinking that I am a bad person and that I don't love Maria, but I do."

"Oh," Jack was relieved because that wasn't at all that he was thinking, and he was happy that at least one person on this island was not a clairvoyant.

"I need to talk to Maria."

"Now?"

"When then? After the wedding?"

"All I can tell you, man, is follow your heart."

***

Nikos was outside tending to the roses next to the door. It looked like he was trying to choose one for tomorrow's wedding; he was sorting through the blossoms and studying them as he went. It was a little difficult to choose since it was almost twilight, so he wanted to go turn the courtyard lights on. As he turned around, he was almost knocked over by Yiorgos, who barged in followed by Jack.

"Sorry, Papa," he said urgently. "Where is Maria?"

"You look so handsome," Nikos said looking up and down at him wearing his new suit and totally ignoring his request.

"I'm going in," he announced once he heard Maria's laughter coming from his mother's workshop.

"You can't," Nikos started to say, but it was too late. Yiorgos was on a mission, and both Nikos and Jack followed.

The only sound that came next was a sigh then deafening silence as the three women stood with open jaws when they saw Yiorgos standing in their midst with Nikos and Jack close behind him. Katherine stood behind Maria, holding the bodice of Maria's wedding dress with both hands to keep it from falling since just moments before the intrusion, she had unzipped it. It looked so awkward to see one woman cupping the breasts of another woman, and the men were definitely awestruck.

"Oh, get over it!" Theodora said as she zipped the dress back up and tried to make light of the situation. "You can take your hands off her breasts now, honey, or my son will get jealous."

Katherine blushed as she quickly removed her hands.

"You! What are you doing here?" Theodora asked with irritation and gave Nikos a mild slap across the face.

"What did you do that for?" Nikos protested. "I was trying to prevent him from coming in! It's your son who needs the slap."

"I will leave my son to his wife to deal with him. In the meantime, you are my husband, and I can slap you as much as I want," Theodora said, still between mixed humor and anger.

She turned to Maria and asked, "Taking notes, girl?"

"We need to talk," Yiorgos finally said softly to Maria.

When he came in, he was determined to spill everything he was discussing with Jack straight away, but once he saw Maria in the wedding dress, his brain took a hike. His heart beats skipped and tripped all over each other. For a moment, he was going to just turn around and leave, just go home and get over it, and tomorrow, this sweet and gorgeous woman would be his. He realized, though, that he still had to deal with tradition, and that was still bothering him. It was those thoughts that restarted his brain.

"You are not supposed to be here," Maria argued, not understanding the reason for the interruption. "And you, and you," she added, pointing to Nikos and Jack.

"I think we should all leave and let them talk," Katherine said and tried to move from behind Maria.

"No, you stay," Maria ordered, and Katherine froze.

"If she stays, Jack stays," Yiorgos said.

"If Theodora stays, I stay," Nikos said next.

"Hey!" Theodora shouted. "All of you out! No one stays! All out!"

They all complied as they knew better than to question or challenge Theodora's final ruling, leaving Yiorgos and Maria to deal with their issues alone. The workshop door was closed, but the reception door stayed open. After they all went out, Theodora and Nikos kept their ears at the door and listened in on their son and his bride. Jack and Katherine stood idly by and didn't know what to do until Theodora noticed them.

"Jack, go to your room and put on your suit," Theodora ordered. "I brought it down and did some alterations on it earlier and sent it back up." Her last order came with a grin, "Katherine, help him."

Theodora and Nikos went back to eavesdropping as Katherine and Jack glanced at each other, smiled, and climbed slowly up to his room. They both looked down once they heard shouting and something breaking inside the room where Maria and Yiorgos were besieged. They saw Theodora firmly preventing Nikos from going in to interfere.

"My last time here ended with a tragedy," Katherine said as Jack opened the door to let her in.

"Just come in with your right foot first and all will be well."

"The Greeks sure have a solution to everything, don't they?" she said and did exactly as he told her as she came into his room for the second time.

It was as if no time had passed since that last night they were together; everything was the same. Everything was in the same exact place. It was as if Jack took a photograph of his room from different angles once and referred back to it every time he made up his room.

Jack walked in and saw his suit hanging on the closet door with a note attached to it. He came closer and read the note:

Put me on.

He looked back curiously at Katherine, who was staring at him.

"Theodora made me write it," she confessed.

"And she sent you up to make sure that it's done."

"You don't have to do it in front of me," she said, blushing.

"You're not shy, are you?" Jack asked coyly as he slowly took off his shirt, leaving his muscled torso exposed.

"No, I'm not," Katherine said, almost choking on her words.

She was so turned on that she couldn't stand looking at him for one more second. Katherine couldn't stand, period. Her legs nearly betrayed her as he pulled his shirt off and revealed his deliciously toned physique in the unintentionally romantic, dimmed light of the room. She turned around and sat on the chair facing the window to avoid the sight that she could no longer subject herself to. She didn't feel embarrassed or shy; she felt that if she didn't turn around, she was going to pounce on him and knock him down and ravish him.

She listened to the sound as he undid his belt then his zipper, and finally the rustle of the fabric as he took his pants off. A wave of heat rushed over her body followed by tingling chills running up her spine. She peeked at his muted reflection in the window, standing practically naked just a few feet behind her. All she wanted was to amass a little bit of courage to turn around and walk towards him, and she was sure that he would be waiting for her with open arms.

Or will he? she wondered. *After I rejected him and after the mess I caused with Aphroditi?*

She turned her head from his reflection as he continued to get dressed in his suit. Her thoughts were cut short when she felt his warm hand touch lightly on her bare shoulder. She turned to look while Jack took two steps back and paused. She looked him up and down from his very serious face to his Olympian god-like stance to his bare feet.

"You should put your shoes on," she said. "That will show if the trousers hang right." She blushed again, not wanting him to know that she was interested in his trousers at all.

"Right," he said. "So tell me about your trip," he added as he fetched his shoes.

Katherine paused for a moment as if in her brain she heard a different question, something to the tone of, *"Shall I take my clothes off or you will undress me yourself as your lips travel from my neck down to my…"*

"Did you go to the Acropolis?" he said, interrupting her previous assumption.

"Oh, yes. It was lovely, I think I saw more archeological sites in the last ten days than I have ever seen in my whole life," she replied.

He stood again in front of her with his shoes on this time. He looked absolutely perfect and breathtaking. She was speechless as she admired him, nodding her approval.

"Stunning," she said, her wide eyes revealing her wonderment as she gazed at him. "I mean the Acropolis," she stammered, though she really meant him but continued to avoid her obvious attraction to him. "You know what I loved most? The fact that I walked on the same paths that the great Greeks of old times did. Let's be honest. I mean, walking in the footsteps of Socrates? How cool is that?"

"All I know is that I know nothing," Jack said to a perplexed Katherine. "That was the most famous saying by Socrates," he explained.

"I know, I know," she said. "At least I know something,"

she laughed and he followed.

Their laughs were interrupted when they heard Maria outside, suddenly shouting Jack's name. They both went out, and once Maria saw them, she ran and tried to get up the stairs. The wedding dress didn't help, and her first couple attempts were unsuccessful. Theodora and Nikos, who already heard all the conversation that took place inside, stood there and acted surprised, although they were not very convincing.

"I will come down," Jack called, sparing Maria her ordeal and also not realizing yet that she was furious.

"You better," Maria shouted and retreated a few steps back.

Yiorgos, Nikos and Theodora were standing in a semi-circle behind Maria and from the look on their faces, not a single one of them was ready to interfere. Jack went down the stairs, followed by Katherine who lifted the hem her blue dress and descended with grace.

"The dress looks wonderful on you," Maria commented, hiding her anger.

"You too," Katherine replied, not realizing herself what was going on. "You look stunning and the dress is glowing in the courtyard lights. You should see yourself from upstairs....I can take a picture if you want."

"Oh! Really?" Maria said with a smile.

"You look beautiful," Jack said as he was two steps short of the courtyard.

Instead of hearing a thank you, he lost his balance from a very strong, unexpected blow to his jaw from Maria's open hand. Despite that he was standing two feet higher than her, Maria was able to reach him and make good contact and knock him to the side.

"No!" was the only objection heard, and it came from Katherine as she hurried down the steps and held Jack from falling.

"You!" Maria shouted. "I knew it was you! Who else other

than you? Who else would put those ideas in Yiorgos head?" She continued screaming at Jack, who was rubbing his cheek as Katherine checked for bleeding. He was speechless as no one came to his defense, and he still didn't comprehend what she was going on about. "Who else other than you, a woman-hating man!"

No one tried to stop her as she charged and retreated, shouting at Jack, one third in Greek, one third in English, and one third in a language Maria only understood. Jack sat on the stairs, caressing his bruised jaw and trying to understand what Maria was ranting about.

"Now because of you, he's not going to marry me anymore!" Maria finally revealed, ending her ten minutes of rage. She then started to sit down on the courtyard floor.

"No you don't!" Theodora shouted. She ran into the reception and got a chair with a cushion on it and put it behind Maria, saving the dress from getting ruined. "Now you can sit." She stepped away muttering and cursing a few words in Greek.

"Can I talk now?" Jack asked but took the permission and continued anyways, looking at Maria as she looked at the ground with tears pouring down her face. "I didn't tell him anything... I just felt that he wasn't sure. That's all. He said he wanted to talk to you, not break off the wedding."

Maria looked up with inflamed eyes. She tried to pounce on Jack, but this time, she was held by Yiorgos. He guided her back into the seat, and after she sat down, he stayed close, still holding her back from attacking Jack.

"You don't want anyone to be happy!" Maria screamed. "Even your own fiancée left you and ran away!"

The blood drained from Jack's face as her words hit him like bullets. Everyone in the group was stunned and remained speechless.

"*Remember Emily*, Jack?" Maria asked with a sneer, continuing her verbal assault on Jack. "What? Did you tell her to run away and never come back? That you were not sure?"

"Enough," Yiorgos said firmly.

"Did you tell her that 'It's not you, it's me' American crap that Yiorgos just told me? That's why she left and never wanted to see your sorry face anymore?"

"Maria, I said enough," Yiorgos repeated and shook Maria, trying to snap her out of her tirade, but Jack didn't say a word.

"Emily died," Theodora said softly.

After that revelation, everything went silent. No breathing, no heartbeats, no words, and no whispers.

Time stopped.

Maria was the first to speak.

"Is that true?" she asked, not believing what she was hearing. Suddenly her tone softened and she leaned forward, touching Jack's face. "I'm so sorry."

"How did you know?" Jack asked as he turned to Theodora.

"I didn't," she confessed. "You just told me."

Katherine only held Jack in her arms and kissed his cheek softly.

"I am so sorry," Maria said and leaned forward and was about to kneel on the ground.

"Freeze!" Theodora shouted. "Either stand up or sit down, but if that dress touches the ground, I will throw you off the cliff."

Maria complied and a burst into laughter that echoed in the courtyard despite the tragedy that was unveiled. Everyone looked around awkwardly, not understanding her outburst.

"What?" Maria asked. "You didn't get it? The dress was a parachute! I will float down like a feather!"

She burst into laughter again, while everyone else remained silent, not appreciating the joke at such a time.

"I knew there was something wrong," Maria said, again breaking the silence. "Now who buys a house and furnishes it, and instead closes it and stays in a hotel for more than two and a half years?"

Everybody knew that she was describing Jack's situation and life on the island.

"You have a house here?" Katherine asked with a surprise, and Jack only nodded.

"Who stays on this island for two and a half years without leaving it for one day at least?" Maria continued. "You don't even go for a swim! Are you afraid that the tide will take you away?"

"Maria," Theodora said sharply, trying to stop her from saying more. "It's not the time."

Maria was showing concern, but everyone knew that she was deflecting from her own problem. It was her wedding that she was mourning, not Jack's dead fiancée. She was transferring her own anger and bitterness onto Jack.

"Maria," Yiorgios said, breaking in. "Jack didn't tell me all I told you inside." He began his confession as he came from behind her and stood next to her. "I made it up…He told me to follow my heart… that's it."

"So your heart doesn't want me? Is this what you are trying to say?"

"No! I want you, but I don't want all this folklore and rituals and traditions. I don't feel that it is my wedding anymore. I feel it is our parents' wedding."

"Why didn't you tell me?"

"Because I didn't want to hurt your feelings…because you seemed to like it."

"But I don't…I thought you liked it…you see, you never complained about it. The only part that I had fun with was the time I spent in Athens with Katherine in the strip club."

"What?" Yiorgos gasped. "You went to a strip club?"

"Oh, grow up," Theodora said. "She's teasing you."

"I want to marry you, Yiorgos, if it is going to be me and you alone without all this fanfare and a thousand people who are going to criticize us no matter what we did. For them, even if we took them for a trip around the moon, they would say that we could have done better."

"So you don't want a big wedding?

"I want to marry you even if we are the only ones there and you are in shorts and flippers and I am in a housedress," Maria said and paused. "Although I like this dress." She patted it gently. "I want to wear it all the time."

"Trust me," Theodora said. "You wouldn't. He will tear it off you the moment you are both alone."

"Woman!" Nikos scolded.

"Oh, shut up, Nikos! You couldn't even wait until we were alone."

"Mama!" Yiorgos shouted.

"Now you two should get married tonight," Theodora announced as everybody looked at her in surprise at such an impossible suggestion. "You are wearing your dress and Yiorgos his suit and your best man too, and Katherine would be your maid of honor. All we need is a priest."

"Father Elias won't do it," Yiorgos said. "He doesn't believe in eloping."

"I know just the one," Nikos said. "Father Nikolaos."

"They said he was bed ridden and always sick," Maria said.

"But he will marry you. He's the one to go to in situations like this," Nikos said. "Just tell him this," he said and whispered something in Yiorgos ear.

"That would definitely work."

"Now go," Theodora shouted.

"How about my parents?" Maria asked with concern. "Who will tell them? And what will they do?"

"I will take care of them," Theodora said. "They will be fine. You get married and go away on your honeymoon." She paused and glanced at Maria. "Just make sure you are pregnant when you come back."

"Ohhhhh!" Maria protested.

"I was just joking, but it would help," Theodora said. "Anyways, go before I change my mind." She turned to Nikos and said, "Get me a bottle of wine and Maria's parents' phone number."

***

"The view was amazing!" Katherine said from the back seat of Yiorgos' car. "To see all of Athens illuminated by candle light, I have never seen something so beautiful."

Maria started to speak but was interrupted again by a very enthusiastic Katherine.

"And did I tell you I watched all this from the top of Mount Lycabettus?"

"A few times," Jack said with a roll of his eyes beside Katherine.

They were on their way to Father Nikolaos, and they mentioned a story about him involving Easter, and before they finished, Katherine took over and started telling them all about her Easter holiday in Athens. It was all too new for her, and she was like a little girl who's seen the county fair for the first time and couldn't stop talking about it. Everybody else had seen it all, many times before, but despite that, they appreciated the distraction.

Once they arrived at Father Nikolaos's house in Oia, they kicked out Jack and Katherine and talked in private. Through the windshield, Yiorgos and Maria were seen talking, arguing, both shedding a few tears, then hugging and kissing. Finally after a few moments of hesitation, the couple got out of the car and led the way towards the priest's house.

The wife of a priest is called *Presbytera*, which is literally *priestess*, the only name used in daily conversation, even by the priest himself, who was called *Presbiteros*. Some Presbytera live their whole life in a place where the community never gets to know their given name. That was the case with Presbyteros Nikolaos's wife of almost fifty years.

In Orthodoxy, a priest has to get married before he becomes a priest, and although divorce and remarrying are allowed among his parishioners, these privileges are denied for him, as well as remarrying after a priestess's death. That makes a Presbytera the most cared for wife in all of Orthodoxy, in particular Father Nikolaos's wife who just opened the door after the third knock.

"We disabled the doorbell so that no one disturbs the priest in the middle of the night," the Presbytera said to the four unexpected guests who were clearly dressed for a wedding.

"But it's only half past seven," Katherine said from behind Maria.

Maria shushed her quickly then Yiorgos spoke. The rest of the conversation carried on in Greek.

"We are so sorry to disturb you, Presbytera, but if we could talk to Presbyteros Nikolaos…We have a very urgent matter that can't wait until morning."

"You're Theodora's son, aren't you?" The Presbytera asked and Yiorgos nodded. "Your mother is a lovely woman. She always comes to visit me, and last week she made Presbyteros a nice cloak for Easter. Your mother is a saint, but you, I haven't seen you in church since last year."

"He has attended," Maria interrupted. "But since Presbyteros Nikolaos got sick, church wasn't fun anymore."

"Fun?" Presbytera asked, frowning at first, pretending that she was upset then she smiled. "You're right."

"I wish I understood one word of what they are saying," Katherine whispered, leaning into Jack who standing next to her.

"I caught a few words, but we are still in the greeting phase," he replied, and they both chuckled.

"Who's that woman with the American boy?" The Presbytera asked. "Is she the one who fell off the donkey?"

"She's the one," Maria said.

"Don't stand in the wind too long, Presbytera," the tired, weak voice of the priest called from inside. "It's a cold night. Whoever it is, let them come tomorrow."

"Bless him. He's always thinking about me," she said sweetly then started to close the door. "Come tomorrow."

"Do you see what I'm wearing?" Maria asked, blocking the door with her hand.

"I'm neither blind nor an idiot," Presbytera began then continued, not allowing anyone else to speak. "You are eloping, and your wedding is tomorrow. I don't know the reasons, but in all my years as Presbytera, and God knows how many couples knocked our doors at night with your same intentions, I have never seen one who had a planned wedding with a man and still wants to elope with the same man the night before. If you brought with you someone other than Theodora's son, it would have made sense. *Kalinichta.*"

The door slammed closed in Yiorgos and Maria's stunned faces. They discussed between themselves what happened and loosely translated to Katherine and Jack what the Presbytera said.

"Does she even have the authority to do that?" Katherine asked. "I mean, shouldn't she let the priest decide what to do?"

As soon as Katherine finished her sentence, the door opened again. The Presbytera eyed everyone and said, "Presbyteros wants to talk to you," and opened the door wide for them to enter.

"This is what Katherine was just saying," Maria said to the Presbytera as they all came in and stood in the middle of the small room.

"Did she?" The Presbytera asked as she eyed Katherine. "I don't like her."

Only Yiorgos and Maria were allowed to enter the priest's bedroom while Katherine and Jack waited in the living room. The house was built into a niche in the cliff, which was a series of caves previously used by ship crews when Oia was a maritime trading power back in the 19th century. The sheltered walls keep both the heat and the cold out and naturally regulate the temperature inside. Despite that, however, the wooden stove was burning, and a kettle with various herbs was boiling. The Presbytera poured Jack and Katherine each a cup of the herbal tea.

"I need sugar with that," Katherine said after she took a sip of the yellowish liquid.

"You'll ruin it," Presbytera said when Jack translated *sugar* in Greek to her, but she brought Katherine a bowl of sugar anyways. She frowned when half of it was shamelessly transferred into her cup.

The priest called his wife in to consult with her while Jack and Katherine were left alone in the living room. The room was so beautifully decorated that Katherine had a very hard time not staring at every single piece in it. Most of the furniture was over fifty years old, and nearly everything was covered with beautifully handmade crocheted pieces; the designs were intricate and mostly white with some lively color splattered elegantly here and there.

What drew her attention the most were not the dozens of Orthodox icons, which was normal in Greek houses and especially a house of a priest, but the photographs that seemed to be present everywhere she looked. The walls, mantels, and table tops were decorated with photographs, many in ornate golden frames. There was even a cabinet that was open and seemed to be overflowing with photographs. Most of the pictures were in black and white, although from the style, almost half were not more than twenty or thirty years old, and the other half was much older.

"The priest's brother is a photographer. He's older than him, and you can still find him in his studio, perched over a picture retouching it," Jack said after he saw the way Katherine was examining the place.

Katherine stood up and took a tour of the room while Jack stayed seated. The pictures were of newborns being baptized or wedding photos of young couples, children in beautiful clothes holding candles, and two dozen large portraits of who she assumed were family members. The largest among the portraits were the ones of the Presbytera and the Presbyteros, taken when they were both much younger. These hung side by side, and below them were three smaller portraits of wedded couples who Katherine assumed were their children.

"This is the best family tree ever," Katherine commented in amazement once she stood in front of the cabinet and saw that the small pictures were arranged in relation to each other.

"It also shows you that all of Santorini is related to each other."

"You startled me. I thought you were still sitting on the couch."

"I sneaked behind you undetected."

"How old is the priest?"

"Ninety or more," Jack guessed. "He is one of the funniest people who you could ever meet, not your typical priest."

"You know him well?"

"Stay long enough on this island and listen to the stories they tell you and soon enough you will know everybody as if you lived your whole life with them."

"It's also an indication for you to leave and find new stories."

Jack didn't reply to Katherine's last observation. He instead went back to the couch and sat down to continue sipping his herbal tea. A couple of minutes later, Katherine joined him.

"Tell me something funny about the priest," she suggested, breaking the awkward silence.

Jack started telling, without hesitation, a few stories about the priest. Most of them were so funny and unexpected of a priest that it made Katherine laugh loudly and her eyes light up, an effect that Jack loved to have on her. It was a sign for him to continue telling her the stories.

One of them he experienced himself and was not relayed to him by someone else. Last August before the priest fell terribly ill, Jack was dragged by Theodora and Nikos to a Sunday Mass that would be followed by the baptism of the son of one of their relatives. The small church was packed, and everyone was at attention during the sermon; however in the middle of the service, as the priest said, "As Christ had risen up to the heavens", he paused, looking out the window. Shocking everyone in attendance, he then said, "The little bastard rose up the tree!" and ran out of the church and grabbed a wooden stick.

Everybody followed him out and saw that he was running after a couple of young boys down the road. There was a fig tree outside the church, and traditionally its fruits were designated only for the priest and he was the only one who picked from the tree once the figs were ripe. The children always walked by and picked one or two, but this time, they wanted all of the fruit, and they timed their raid at the time of the Mass, assuming that the priest couldn't do anything about it.

"Isn't cursing a sin? Yet doing it inside of a church and by a priest?" Katherine commented after laughing.

"He was always like that, but everybody loved him because he was nice and funny, and they accepted his flaws."

"He used to skip big chunks of the very long sermon on cold days so as not to make people uncomfortable," Jack added. "Once an old woman kept badgering him, telling him that he skipped this and that in the middle of the service. He stopped and told her in the middle of Mass, 'You have a few days left. Spend them with your grandchildren, not listening to me repeating the same words every Sunday.'"

"He was absolutely right," Katherine said.

"Very down to earth," Jack said then turning again to the pictures, he added, "I guess you have a big collection of pictures yourself form all your journeys."

"I have a couple of hundred, yes," she said. "But I haven't been to a place that hasn't been photographed to death before, including this place."

"True. I am sure I'm in more than a dozen tourist photos without me knowing, since almost a million photographs are taken of this island alone every year."

"Impressive. You're famous," she joked and bumped his elbow with hers. "I collect SIM cards and phone cards."

Katherine saw a strange look on Jack's face then explained.

"You know, with every carrier in every country I visited, they package it in a different way. Some I just buy to keep without even opening them."

"That's so unique."

"I have almost a hundred, a full bag."

"That's your legacy."

"That's my baggage," she joked with a hint of realization in her voice.

"Come," The Presbytera said, standing at the bedroom door, cutting into Jack and Katherine's conversation.

Jack looked at her and pointed to himself; she nodded and pointed to both him and Katherine. She turned around and went back in. Katherine put down her extra-sweet cup of herbal tea and followed Jack into the bedroom.

The room was small with a minimalist touch and with more icons than in ten churches combined. The priest was sitting in bed with his snow white beard reaching way down his chest. Since he wasn't wearing anything on his head, Katherine noticed that his hair was gathered in a bun behind his head in the old tradition of the Orthodox clergy not to cut their beards or hair. To her, he looked a bit like an Old World Santa Claus, less the red coat and Christmas cheer, though she didn't dare speak it.

Jack said good evening in great courtesy as the priest ordered everyone to switch places. The Presbytera brought him his hat and a piece of cloth to wear around his neck. His face lit up when Katherine smiled at him. Despite his old age and frail body, he seemed to have serene features that emitted peace and love with great command.

The ceremony ended in less than one minute, in great contrast to the one-and sometimes two-hour long church wedding that Maria and Yiorgos would have endured if they had waited till tomorrow. Maria was nice enough to translate to Katherine and Jack what was the priest saying. He ended the ceremony by saying, "That will do for tonight. We will continue some other time, and you may kiss the bride."

The four left soon after Katherine and Jack declined the priest's generous offer to wed them since he was awake and he had his priesthood gear on. The Presbytera offered them some sweets and sent them off. Jack and Katherine had to wait for the newlyweds until they finished their proper kiss outside the priest's house rather than the shy peck they took inside.

"Now that's a real kiss," Maria said and then came running and hugged Katherine.

"I liked the sweet wine that they made us drink. Can we go back and ask them for more?" Katherine asked, referring to the sip of wine they were offered during the ceremony.

"I want to go sip on my husband's lips," Maria said without any hint of shame.

Jack drove this time with Katherine beside him, and the newlyweds sat in the back. The drive was a short trip down the hill, but instead, Jack took them on a short tour of the island. The music coming from the radio that Katherine turned on slightly masked the sounds of the lovers' kisses and giggling coming from the back seat. Maria and Yiorgos didn't seem very interested in the tour or conscious that there was someone else other than them in the car.

The tour lasted only half an hour, and soon enough, for the sake of everybody, the car was parked a short walk before the steps leading to the port of Armeni, located under the cliffs of Oia. Maria and Yiorgos were supposed to take a sail boat around the islands for their honeymoon. They would be leaving tomorrow, instead of a few days later as originally planned.

"You can both come if you want," Maria offered to Yiorgos's horror. "What, darling? There are two cabins, and they can put in earplugs," she said playfully.

"You know, tradition says that you have to carry your bride over the steps," Jack said referring to the 275 steps leading down to the port and ignoring Maria's invitation.

"You can have her in this case," Yiorgos said jokingly and pushed Maria away.

"No, you don't! You have duties to perform," Maria said, jumping into Yiorgos arms.

"Now you two go make some waves," Katherine said walking closer and giving Maria and Yiorgos each a kiss.

Yiorgos carried Maria over the first step only. Once her feet were on the ground again and with her back to Katherine, she shouted her name and threw the bouquet that Nikos prepared and that she had been holding all this time. Katherine and Jack both caught it at the same time. With their faces so close and their lips almost touching, they looked in each other's eyes in silence as Maria's and Yiorgos's laughs and giggles echoed through the night as they descended the stairs.

"I think we should go," Jack said.

"Wait! I need to ask Yiorgos one more thing," Katherine said and ran towards the stairs and shouted. "What did you say to the priest to convince him to marry you tonight?"

"I told him what my dad told me to say," Yiorgos shouted back. "If you don't marry us tonight, I will convert to Catholicism."

All I Know is that I Know Nothing

"That's the house you stopped and stared at when we came here together," Katherine said as Jack parked the car on the steep road.

"We don't have to do this," Jack said when Katherine opened her door and started to get out.

"We totally have to! Come on. We came all this way. I want to see the inside!"

Katherine didn't give him any chance to protest. She got out and walked ahead of him all the way to the blue wooden gate guarding the house.

A light breeze carried the fresh smell of jasmine and encircled Katherine as she opened the gate and stepped into the small courtyard. Her move enticed Jack to hesitantly get out of the car and walk towards her. She didn't wait for him and used the street light to help her climb the twenty steps towards the house entrance. The way up was through a tunnel of fragrant pink flowers arching overhead; it was like passing through a fog of sweet perfume. Katherine was enchanted by the atmosphere, and she thought how lucky Emily was to have had Jack do all this for her.

With that thought, he appeared at the bottom of the steps. She didn't say a word, she just waited. A minute passed, and he didn't come up, then two minutes, then three. Katherine looked around her and saw three small flower pots on the ground. She lifted the first one, then the second one, and under the third one, she found a key.

Without looking down at Jack, she tried the key in the door, and it worked. Without a shred of hesitation, she opened the door and went in. The inside was pitch black except for the faint light coming through the door. She grasped at the walls and found the light switch then flipped it on and off and on several times, but nothing happened.

"The electricity is turned off," Jack said quietly as he put his hand over hers. "It doesn't matter how many times you try the switch, it's not gonna work."

His touch was light, and he whispered his words. It was like he was trying his best not to disturb the people sleeping in the house. Instead he was trying not to disturb the past, not to awaken it, a past that he put to sleep almost three years ago. Instead, his soft touch over Katherine's hand and the whispers in her ears awakened feelings that she forgot a long time ago. All she wanted to do was to turn around and kiss his lips in the darkness, but she couldn't, at least not yet.

Jack used the light from the door and his knowledge of the place to navigate his way towards the windows. He opened the first one, then the second, then the third. The squeaks echoed all over the house and throughout the calm neighborhood. The beams of light and its resulting shades and shadows revealed a fully furnished room, yet everything was covered with ghostly white linen cloths.

"Did Emily ever see this?" Katherine asked after closing the door behind her and stepping to the middle of the room.

Jack didn't say a word; he just shook his head. He came and stood next to Katherine and took the hand that had the key in it. She opened her hand, and the key slipped from her hand into his and onto the marble floor. The antique metal key landed with a quiet clatter, yet Jack trembled as if he heard the sound of thunder.

Katherine reached for his hand in the darkness and pulled him behind her. Jack followed her as she entered the next room. A crack in the shutters guided her towards the window. She released Jack's hand and opened the window. The light on this side of the house was dimmer, but she could see what seemed to be a bed, also covered with sheets of white linen.

Jack was only one step away, watching her. She turned towards him and covered the distance between them. She took his hands in hers then she lifted herself up and brought her lips to his. His lips trembled at her touch then warmed as they met hers softly. His kiss became more intent as he took her lips between his. Then and there she knew how much she loved him, how much he meant to her, and how fast he made her heart beat.

Katherine knew how much Jack was capable of doing when he loved someone. He had created for Emily a home, a kingdom of her own, and kept it for her even after she was gone. He imprisoned himself on an island, surrounded by the deep sea while her spirit soared up in the sky and roamed around free. The depth of his commitment to a ghost and his choice to live a life so secluded would seem eccentric, self-serving, or even a little bit crazy to some, but Katherine could see that he was a man made out of love and devotion. At that moment, she felt herself even more drawn to him than she had ever been. She surrendered herself to his kiss then almost instantly he pulled away.

"Let me go find a candle," Jack said softly as their lips parted.

"Don't be long," Katherine said, letting his hands go.

His hand left the warmth of hers, and he turned around and walked away. For the first time, part of him was left with a woman other than Emily, and he took with him Katherine's kisses, touches, and heartbeats. He stopped and looked back and Katherine's face was still there, waiting and smiling at him before he turned and left the room. She hadn't disappeared. Her softness and tenderness was still there, waiting to envelop him like a welcoming blanket of warmth and security.

Although it was dark, his memory of the house that he visited every day since Emily left was impeccable. The only day that he didn't visit was the day that Katherine left. Every day he would come, pass by the house to water the flowers or go inside and walk around. Like a man possessed, he would silently traverse the house, seeming to take a silent inventory or pausing to reposition an object just so, although nothing had been moved since his last visit. No dust settled on the tabletops nor did the house have the stale smell of a house abandoned.

Guided by the scent of vanilla and beeswax, he found a few scented candles on a shelf. The matchbox wasn't too far away either. Darkness turned into light, a soft glow that guided him back to the bedroom. The cold walls of the vacant house took on a warm and intimate glow in the candlelight, and shadows danced like fairies across the room.

Jack stood in the bedroom doorway looking in. The candle's flame flickered in the soft breeze that came through the open window, almost extinguishing it before Jack protected it by putting his palm in front of it. Katherine wasn't there. He looked closer, taking his hand off the light's path and still she wasn't there. He took a couple of steps, and he saw that the bed was uncovered. The white linen sheet had given way to a plush crimson duvet; he frowned because he knew that he had left the linens in place over all of the furniture in the house. He took another step forward and was about to call Katherine's name when he heard her.

Jack...

Digging deep into his memory, he couldn't recall hearing his name spoken in such a way. It sounded so mesmerizingly soft. It was more of a whisper of a breath than a spoken word. It was the breath of life and love as she exhaled one simple word, but it was the first word either spoke after he brought the candle and the last that would be spoken until dawn.

He turned around and still couldn't see her. He extended the candle before him at the same moment that she emerged from the darkest corner of the room into the light. Even though he was expecting her, he was startled by her exquisite beauty as the candlelight illuminated her naked body, highlighting parts and shadowing others. Her skin was luminous as she approached him, the curves of her body a divine vision of perfection and femininity.

Jack was mesmerized, awestruck, and fascinated all at once. He just wanted to look at her all night long, a real Venus, a work of art, who was standing mere steps away from him. His heartbeat raced, like it did in the heart of primal men for hundreds of thousands of years before him. Fight or flight.

Katherine walked closer to him as he remained motionless. He couldn't have moved even if he tried to. His eyes were glued to her as she silently approached, gliding across the floor like an angel on gossamer wings. She was now a few inches away. He could feel her breath on him, he could feel her warmth and her love, hear her heart beating in rhythm with his, and he could even read her thoughts. She looked into his eyes, to read all of his unspoken words, and all she could see was her own reflection shimmering in his eyes. There was no denying that he wanted her as much as she wanted him.

She took the candle from his quivering hand and set it down on the floor. Her fingers unbuttoned his shirt, her movements graceful, revealing his toned, muscled chest. She leaned forward into him as the shirt dropped, easing her feminine curves against his strong male form. The moment that their naked bodies touched, a spark ignited not only in their bodies but in their hearts. They fed on each other's warmth; when their souls collided, their fusion created a light that brightened the darkness of their lives. It broke down the protective walls that they had both built around themselves, their defenses crumbling like the ancient ruins. It was the moment their world was created.

Jack's hand slowly trailed down Katherine's neck, down her spine, and settled onto the small of her back. She kissed the palm of his hand that lay on her cheek, the one upon which Cassandra has seen such devastation, as if she knew and was trying to heal him. The gaze of his eyes magically pulled her up on her toes as he lifted her chin. His lips brushed hers tentatively then her soft lips surrendered to his firm kiss and parted defenselessly for his tongue to charge forward seeking hers.

The winds of lust blew the candle light away.

Oh, if the sheets on that bed could speak, they would recite the most beautiful poetry ever written. If they could sing, they would chant the most melodious ballads. If they could see, they would blush as crimson as the duvet that had been pulled aside as he guided her to the bed. If they could feel, they would moan with desire and lust as Jack and Katherine's bodies joined at long last. The silky sheets spread and crumpled beneath them as they fell weak and helpless into the arms of the love that they had both shielded themselves from and wrestled against for so long.

Oh, the softness of her skin touched by the tips of his fingers. He studied the sleek, velvet canvas of her body as a blind man seeking the meaning of Life. Every spot, every hill and valley, every curve was marked as his by the soft caresses of his lips. He gripped the delicate flesh of her hips as their bodies danced together, her moans of pleasure gently muffled as she softly bit his lips.

Oh, the light of dawn breaking in, like the parting of clouds after a thunderstorm. The gods and goddesses of love sent their warm rays bouncing off of the lovers' gleaming skin. In the aftermath of their tempest, Jack and Katherine lay entangled in each other, the silken sheets draped carelessly over their bodies. They lay blissful in the tranquility of the ultimate consummation of their passions, breathless, vulnerable, their love now exposed to the morning sun and to the world to see.

***

Katherine opened her eyes upon a smiling face beside her, rough with the emerging spikes of one-day unshaven skin but softened by love. Jack looked serene, happy, satisfied, and hopeful. Her gaze studied him from head to toe as he lay beside her. She adored every inch of him, from his handsome face to his tender lips, from his strong, protective arms to his gentle yet masculine hands. Her lips had nibbled his ears and inhaled the deep masculine scent of his neck; her tongue had tasted the sweet saltiness of his skin as they made love. Her eyes traveled the landscape of his body from his chest to his belly, descending to his manhood and down his legs to the tips of his toes. His body, his heart, his soul, and even his breath belonged to her, and she smiled softly, unable to find the words to express any of what she felt in that moment.

"Stop staring at me," Jack said with his eyes still shut.

"How did you know I was staring at you?"

"I felt your eyes on me."

"Did you feel this on you too?" Katherine asked before quickly flipping Jack on his back and laying over him, kissing his lips deeply.

"Mmmmmmm," all was that came from between Jack's lips.

Katherine's naked body straddling Jack's reignited their desires. It was just an hour ago when their bodies detached from their all-night lovemaking marathon. It seemed that their desire had exceeded the limits of biology, chemistry, math, physics, astronomy, and logic, in all of which the ancient Greeks excelled. They were not on the island of Santorini anymore; they had crossed oceans of time and space and washed ashore on the island of Katherine and Jack.

"I have to tell you something," Katherine said half an hour later as she lay on her side with Jack hugging her from behind.

"Speak."

"First, you have to stop kissing my neck. Can you do that?"

She paused for a few seconds as Jack complied then his fingers traveled from her thigh up to her hip and back down again.

"And caressing my butt," she said with a giggle.

Katherine peeled herself off Jack, sat up in bed, and pulled her knees to her chest, holding herself tightly. Jack watched her beautiful face change from serene to serious. She sat quiet as she looked at a virtual point in mid-air then she finally started talking.

"I was just out of college…Mom and Dad were back together, and I was looking for a job. One day, a friend of mine was showing a house to some guy. It was in Palo Alto…A big five-bedroom house, six bathrooms, a pool, and the whole nine yards."

Jack's hand didn't stay away for long. As soon as Katherine started telling him her story, he turned on his belly and extended his hand to settle on her waist. She released her legs then he cradled his head in her lap and listened carefully to what she was saying.

Katherine met her friend's client, who easily parted with a few million dollars to buy that house. While she and her friend Lillian were out celebrating the sale, he called and asked Katherine out. Katherine didn't accept the first time, but after his insistence, she accepted to go out with him for dinner.

Jeremy was in his late 40s, elegant, decisive, and preoccupied with his work. He climbed the success ladder after he moved to Silicon Valley from Los Angeles in the 1980's, the Golden Age of tech companies. He seemed ready to settle down and have someone to share his success. After a few dates, he unexpectedly proposed to

Katherine.

"It was more like a business proposal than a marriage proposal," Katherine said, caressing Jack's hair.

A couple of months later, they got married, despite the disapproval of her dad. Her father thought that Jeremy was looking more for a trophy wife than for someone to share a life with.

"He asked me, 'How is he gonna call me Dad and I am the same age as him?'" Katherine said, injecting some humor in an otherwise serious story.

Jeremy was busy all the time; they even had a very short honeymoon in nearby Hawaii so that he wouldn't miss much time monitoring stocks and startups. It wasn't the romantic life that Katherine read and dreamed about, but it was what she chose and she was going to make the best of it. She tried to make him come home for dinner and stay off work for the weekends by planning exciting menus, activities, and wearing attractive outfits and lingerie. He didn't abide by her wishes most of the time, but once in a while, life wasn't all work for him.

Dinners out were reserved to serve a business purpose. He wore her on his arm like he wore his diamond studded cufflinks, just as her dad had suspected he would. He took his trips alone and left her for days in a big empty house, a lonely queen. She tried to work, but he always convinced her off it, saying that he earned plenty of money to more than take care of them both and then some. He bought her gifts and gave her free reign of her own credit card, as if that would keep her satisfied.

"'You have two servants, a cook, and a driver,' he used to tell me," Katherine remembered. "Go shopping, no need to work, leave it to me."

Her dad and mom felt her pain, despite the fact that she tried to hide it from them, but remained silent to spare her from the "I told you so" lecture. Jeremy, after all, wasn't a bad man, she convinced herself; he was rather a busy man, something that she discovered was totally wrong years later.

"Our sex life was scheduled like everything else in Jeremy's life," she said and then regretted saying it to the man that she just had the most passionate lovemaking of her life with.

Rare were the moments when they had real fun at home together as a couple or outside the home. Only a couple of times a year, they would go out to have non-work related fun, not a ballgame sponsored by some company Jeremy had invested in.

"He was programmed for work," she said. "People who were programmed for life have a drink at ten in the morning and say that it's five PM somewhere, but Jeremy used to keep working until midnight, saying that the market opening bell is ringing somewhere."

Katherine leaned over and gave Jack a kiss on his cheek. His hand caressed her hair, and for a moment, all she wanted was to fall back into his arms and make love to him until nightfall, but she had to release her demons first and complete what she started. She had to get it off her chest and clear her heart of the old pains to make way for new love to enter it.

"He was an *askhole*. He used to wake me up at six in the morning to ask me what tie to wear then pick a totally different one," Katherine said.

"*Askhole?*" Jack asked curiously, not sure if he heard her right.

"Yeah, someone who constantly asks for your advice and always does the opposite of what you told them," Katherine explained. "It wasn't only with ties. It was with everything. It was as if he did it on purpose just to make me feel that I make bad choices."

She paused thoughtfully for a moment and cleared her throat.

"He was right," she said with a sigh. "I made wrong choices, and the first one was him."

Jack turned over to face her and lifted his head up. He found her lips and gave her a long kiss as tears filled her eyes and fell over his face. She kissed him back, and his sweet breath gave her the courage she needed to continue.

At first, she was upset when Jeremy told her that he didn't want any children. She tried unsuccessfully to convince him otherwise. She almost got herself pregnant without his approval but aborted her plans after her mother told her that she would bear and raise a child who would be resented by his father, and that wouldn't be healthy for her or the baby. Two years into their marriage, she decided to take all the precautions available for her not to have Jeremy's offspring.

In September 2001, Jeremy took Katherine with him on a business trip to New York. She had never been to the Big Apple, so she was excited to go, even though she had to see the city on her own except for a couple of dinners where she had to be Jeremy's accessory. She was happy to be free from his reign and reveled in her freedom, and in two days and three nights, she saw two Broadway shows, a ball game, visited three different museums, ate at five different restaurants, and listened and danced to live jazz music all night long. She saw Jeremy a total of three and a half hours during the trip, and even that was much more than she desired.

"Next morning, I was about to leave the hotel to get some breakfast and go see Lady Liberty when all hell broke out," Katherine said. The blood drained from her face as she recalled what happened next.

Jack sprang up from the bed when he heard her next words.

"It was the morning of September 11th."

Katherine was startled by Jack's reaction. It was so sudden and unexpected. He started pacing back and forth as she watched him. His naked body was not there anymore. All she could see were his naked emotions trying to escape out of him. Katherine decided to continue and hoped that the recollection of that day's memory would bring her some peace.

Her hotel suite had a direct view of the Twin Towers, *The Pillars of Capitalism,* as Jeremy used to call them. He specifically asked and insisted on the view when he booked that suite a month ago, a view that changed from a symbol of pride and prosperity to shock and tragedy in just a few seconds. A thick black cloud rose from the North Tower as it burned.

It was just before nine, and she immediately ran for the phone. No matter how many times she tried, she was never able to get through to Jeremy. She had started to panic then she heard an urgent knocking on her door. She didn't respond at first then the knock became louder and then someone barged through the door. It was an officer of the hotel security staff who was making sure that she was ok. He verified her name on a list and told her it was better to stay away from the windows for her own safety.

Katherine was standing next to the door after seeing the officer out when the earth shook the second time. This time it was stronger, and the window shattered but stayed in place. She was thrown forward but managed to keep her balance. She turned around, and this time, in her direct view, the South Tower was burning.

She was panic-stricken as the security staff came back in, and this time, she was quickly escorted to the lobby. It was a chapter of the apocalypse. They used the stairs, so it took them a while to reach ground level due to the sheer volume of people being evacuated; some of them were still in their morning robes.

"Some of the women didn't even have time to wear makeup or do their hair, let alone put on their Blahnik's," Katherine said, finding a way to insert some black humor in a tragedy.

Jack sat down on the floor across from her. He wasn't looking at her, and it seemed that he was distracted by distant thoughts, but Katherine knew that he was listening to every word she said.

Santorini

After spending more than four hours watching the tragedy unfold and repeated again and again on the TV screens in the hotel's conference room where most of the guests were, Katherine saw Jeremy arrive. She ran to him when she saw him and hugged him closely, although he was all covered with dust. As she clung to her husband, who until then she hadn't been sure if he was dead or alive, all he said to her in an irritated tone was that he needed a shower.

Jeremy bribed a security guard who was supposed not to let anyone go up to their rooms and took Katherine and went up to their suite. He took a shower while Katherine waited on him. He was telling her that he had a breakfast meeting at Windows on the World restaurant at the top floor of the North Tower, but his guest called to tell him as he was entering the building that he was already there. The first plane struck just as he was about to step into the elevator.

It took him some time to know what was happening, and when he did, he was so thankful that he wasn't the first one to arrive that day. Without an ounce of compassion, he kept talking about how luck was on his side and how invincible he felt for staying alive.

"He said that he felt that he was Superman," Katherine said with disdain. "He didn't have one thread of empathy towards the people who died and the tragedy that was unfolding."

Jack shook his head sorrowfully as Katherine continued.

"The man who he was meeting had a wife and three children, and when I pointed that out to Jeremy, all he said was that he was sure that he had enough life insurance coverage for them to live comfortably for many years to come."

Katherine paused and swallowed hard.

"It was then that I realized that I had married a heartless monster," Katherine whispered, fighting a tear. "I can take anything but that."

"Jeremy went on and on, saying how disastrous it was that the Stock Exchange was going to be closed and that all the suckers would sell their stocks once it reopened and what a great opportunity it would be to start buying on the cheap and later sell once the stocks soared." Katherine remembered angrily. "All he was thinking was how much he could profit from the tragedy of others. All I wanted was to be away from him, as far away as possible."

Katherine came and sat at the edge of the bed facing Jack.

"I didn't sleep that night, and in the morning, I packed just one small bag, and I left before he even woke up. It took me two hours to reach uptown, and I will never forget the faces that I saw on my way there. It was like the End of Days."

Katherine wanted to fly away on the first flight to anywhere away from Jeremy, but all the airports were shut down. She wanted to get as far away from him as she could, but instead she stayed in a hotel uptown. Jeremy called her cell, and she told him that she left for good. He didn't understand why, and he didn't ask her why. He simply didn't care.

"Maybe he thought that if a woman decided to leave him, it would be her loss," Katherine said, again trying to find some dark humor amidst the ruins of her past.

Katherine was able to contact her parents who were worried sick, and she told them that it was over between her and Jeremy. He father said that his relief was double because she was alive and free from the man who stole her smile. She told them that she planned on going home, her real home, once she could get a flight out.

"I was at the airport a week later, waiting to board a flight to San Francisco when I looked at my two years old passport and saw that all its pages were empty," Katherine continued. "It was just like my life, blank."

"I bought a ticket to Paris, France, called my parents and told them about my plans, and went on the journey of my life, a journey that took me across the world to places that I have only seen in pictures and places that had never been photographed before."

She reached out and caressed his cheek, but he was still focused away from her.

"A journey that brought me here…to you."

Jack didn't respond.

"This is me," she said, after emptying her soul to him. "All bared and naked to you."

Jack still didn't look at her, but it seemed that he was ready to speak and she was ready to listen after saying one last thing.

"There are three strong feeling that humans can hold towards each other," she said as she held his hand.

"Love, which is strong and gives your soul moments of joy and someone to wait for and something to look forward to…Hate, which is stronger than love and makes you want to hurt someone and make them suffer, but you still think of them day and night…But the strongest feeling of all is indifference…when you stop caring and stop aspiring, and a person that you might love or hate becomes a nobody and every memory, good or bad of him, is wiped out of your soul."

Katherine's last statement grabbed Jack's attention. He turned towards her and looked into her. He saw the woman who picked up a great viewpoint not by walking in the footsteps of ancient philosophers but by living it herself.

"This is the first time I told anyone about my life and how I became and why I became me," she confessed then paused. "What made you who you are today, Jack?"

Her deep stare into his eyes rendered him self-conscious but also gave him the courage to speak. He also felt safe with her, especially when she turned to face him and took him gently into her loving embrace. They sat entwined in each other's arms, and she laid her head on his shoulder while her hand caressed his bare back.

Entangled, they both felt the rush of intimacy and the urge to make love again. It came so natural to them and so intuitive that it felt as if their bodies were a part of one heart separated many years ago and now reunited. Their hands, lips, and skin were beyond exploring to find the right spots. Their bodies moved together instinctively, caressing like old lovers with an intimate knowledge of every erogenous zone and fused together in love.

They lay breathless on the floor, neither one minding the cold. Katherine rested on top of Jack, listening to his heartbeats decelerating from their peak moments ago. The sound was hypnotic, and it took her to another place as her heart beat in rhythm with his and the rate of their breathing coincided. For a moment, she didn't realize that Jack was talking to her or what was he saying.

"What?" Katherine asked.

"Emily was Chad The Angry Guy's daughter," Jack repeated as Katherine perked up and looked up at him then settled again on his chest.

They met when Jack's mom sent him to retrieve his dog, which was coincidentally named Chad, from his front yard and to apologize to him. He was dreading having to talk to Chad The Angry Guy, so he was surprised when he arrived and a girl his age had befriended his dog and was playing with him. He was jealous at first because he didn't want his dog to like anyone but him, but soon he didn't mind sharing his dog's loyalty with the sweet girl.

Jack and Emily grew up to become very good friends, and they spent so much time together that their whereabouts became so predictable to the point that when she wasn't at home, her parents knew that she was at Jack's place, and when he wasn't home, his parents knew that he was at Emily's. Everyone was surprised that all these years, their relationship never switched from friendship into romance. They even double-dated in high school and all through college.

It wasn't until after Jack's return from Silicon Valley that their love spark was ignited. Emily was living and working in downtown

Manhattan, and Jack had just moved back home with his parents. They missed each other dearly when they were apart and she was elated when he moved back to the old neighborhood. Emily came every weekend to see her parents and catch up with her best friend.

She was supportive through his depression after losing everything when his company suddenly went under. She was the first one to suggest that he should go back to writing. She loved the short stories he used to write when they were younger and how they used to pretend to be private investigators partners like Laura Holt and Remington Steele. One night when Emily was reading one of Jack's love scenes in his manuscript, she felt that Jack was describing her and she felt that the love scene was a substitute for making love to her. It was as if years of yearning for each other had been kept simmering beneath the surface and suddenly boiled to the surface.

She came to his house and climbed to his room in the middle of the night as she had many times in their childhood and teen years. He was asleep, and she slipped quietly into his bed beside him. As if he sensed her presence, he instantly woke and turned to her. Neither of them said a word; they only fell into a passionate kiss, and as surprised as he was at her sudden appearance in his room, they made love all night long. Just like that, they became a couple. A couple who months later, on the day that Jack received the good news that his book was going to be published, they announced their engagement.

Emily and Jack were living a dream. Even before his book was published, he signed a six-figure movie deal. The studio sent him on a private jet to Los Angeles for a signing ceremony, and he took Emily with him. She took a couple of days off work, and they enjoyed the Mediterranean weather of sunny California.

It was then that the idea of moving to southern Europe came to them. They first thought of Nice then thought of Sicily, and then they met a movie executive who was raving about the time he spent in Greece and how much he loved the islands and he couldn't stop talking about Santorini. By the time they came back from California, their mind was set on where they would be spending the next phase of their lives.

Since neither of them had visited that part of the world before, they decided to go on a trip. Their trip was scheduled in late spring, but once Jack's book was released, he had to go on a book tour for a couple of months, and their trip was postponed until midsummer. What was supposed to be a two-week exploratory trip was extended to a month.

Emily called her company and informed them that she was resigning, so they urged her to take the extra two weeks to think about it before making her final decision. Jack's book was doing great, and the studio announced that they would start casting in early October. The first draft of his second book was due in a month, but he had already completed it in the first two weeks he and Emily spent on Santorini. Despite the distractions, this magnificent place was a real inspiration.

They decided to buy a house and move permanently onto the fabulous island. They looked around and found a house on Oia and immediately fell in love with it. The house belonged to Maria's grandparents. Emily called her parents and informed them about her decision, and Jack told his mother to prepare herself to travel in mid-September to attend his wedding.

Amidst her company's insistence, Emily flew back to New York for a week to insure a smooth transition of her duties to one of her colleagues who took over her job. In the meantime, she could look for a wedding dress and come back with her parents and with Jack's mother to Santorini. Jack stayed behind on the island and made sure that the house was perfect and all the preparations for the wedding were completed.

"I came back from my afternoon swim when I saw a bunch

of people huddled around a TV in a seaside café," Jack said as the tone of his voice changed. "I didn't know what it was all about until I came closer. I had a direct sight of the screen just as I saw a plane hitting the World Trade Center."

Katherine, who was listening with her eyes closed as she rested her head on his chest, suddenly lifted her head and opened her eyes wide. In a second, she understood everything. Jack didn't have to continue. She already knew how he lost Emily. A tear came down her cheek as she watched his face. He wanted to continue, but she placed her index finger over his lips as that tear splashed onto his face.

Tears welled up in his eyes when he realized that she already knew, that she already saw, and that she already understood his pain and what was he going through. His tears mixed with hers as they wept together. It was a rare moment for him; the last time he cried was when his father died.

"I knew she was gone," Jack said minutes later and wept uncontrollably as Katherine held him tight.

While Katherine left Jeremy by choice, Emily was snatched away from Jack by the forces of evil. While Katherine ran free roaming all over the earth, basking in the light of independence, Jack was trapped inside a prison that was once his and his Emily's paradise.

Jack never knew what exactly happened to Emily; the pain in his heart only told him that she was gone. He never contacted her parents, although they tried to call him. Receiving the call was enough to verify what he already knew in his heart. The other half of his soul had left this earth, and he was devastated. He never discussed it with his mom either, although she tried several times to bring it up. Jack never talked about Emily ever again until today. The few people who knew her on the island were ignored when they asked him about her. Soon they all thought that the marriage had been canceled, and they didn't discuss it any further.

Jack was practically in hell. He was desperate, desolate, and had turned to alcohol to ease his pain, only to have it come back to haunt him even more. Her ghost haunted him with or without the alcohol, so he cleaned himself up and focused intently on his writing. Over time, he kept himself in the solitude of the island, never leaving it and told himself that his isolation was required for his work and was not a self-inflicted purgatory.

Until today.

Today he realized that Emily was really gone. His words and tears freed her spirit, and it flew away to its final resting place. He just realized that he would never meet her again, that no matter how much time he stayed, she would never be back.

The time that stopped on that dreadful day leaped forward and suddenly jolted him into the present. It hit him like an electric shock, and the impact nearly knocked Katherine off as he jumped away. She remained calm and caressed his cheek. He was cold, and his entire body was quivering. She stood up and brought a blanket from the cabinet and covered him with it.

Katherine paused for a moment. Her beautiful naked body towering over him, she looked down deeply into his face. Behind all the masks he wore and the facades and walls he had built around himself, she saw love. She shivered and picked up her dress from the pile of their discarded clothing and started putting it on.

"Don't go," he whispered, barely able to force out the words.

Jack was in love, vulnerable and afraid. He realized now what Katherine meant to him and his fear of losing her took over his body and soul. He was afraid that she would go and never come back again like Emily did, and Katherine knew that.

"Come with me," she said.

"There is nothing out there for me."

"There will be me," she said, zipping up her dress.

Santorini

She sat on the bed, putting her shoes on. Jack didn't move; he was still sitting on the floor covered with the blanket. She didn't want to leave him like that, but she also didn't want to fall victim to the trap of the island's allure. She could always stay, but Santorini, although magnificent, was someone else's dream. She already did that years ago and lived someone else's life and finally regained her freedom and ran away. Today she was free, and she wanted to go home.

Jack watched her silently as she got herself ready. When she stood over him and pleaded one last time for him to come with her, she extended her hand to him, and he grabbed it. He tried to pull her down and told her to stay, begged her not to go. He was tearful and desperate, but Katherine managed to escape from his grip and ran to the door, fighting her own tears. He bolted to his feet and ran after her. She opened the door and stood in it. Jack stopped a few feet away from her, beautiful and naked in the morning light, body and soul.

"Stay," he begged in one final desperate plea.

He reached a trembling hand out to her, certain that she would take it, but she didn't.

"Goodbye," she whispered as tears spilled down her cheeks. She quickly turned and ran down the stairs and disappeared into the labyrinth of narrow streets.

Jack froze in his place, in shock that Katherine had left him once again. He dropped to the floor and cradled his head in his hands in front of the open door. He sobbed uncontrollably, weighed down by a billion thoughts and the heaviness of her departure.

***

It was a very calm Sunday. The streets were almost deserted, and the morning cacophony of church bells had long since given way to the few birds chirping around enjoying a warm spring morning. Half of Santorini was attending Mass, and the other half was sleeping off Saturday night's drunken party. All that came to Jack's advantage since he was driving back to the hotel under the influence of Katherine's departure and he wasn't much aware of his surroundings. Empty roads were very much appreciated.

Jack arrived at the hotel almost an hour after Katherine departed his house. After a long period of inner calm where his brain took a time out and his eyes kept staring at the open door, the sun rays beat down on him. He literally saw the light. He got up, put his clothes on, and drove back to the hotel. He didn't water the plants like he did every day. He locked the door, put the key in his pocket, and ran down to the car.

"*Kalimera sas,*" he said as he entered from the main gate, surprised to see Nikos and Theodora drinking coffee in the courtyard. "What are you doing here?"

"Fishing," Theodora answered sarcastically. "What do you see us doing?"

"I meant, you were supposed to be at church," Jack backed off.

"We decided to wait this one out," Nikos said. "You know!"

"Wait! I will get you a cup from inside," Theodora said and started to get up.

"I don't want any coffee."

"You know it's impolite to say that."

"Ok, I'm sorry," Jack said. "I will go get a cup," and went in to bring a cup.

He came back five seconds later without a cup in his hand.

"What is Katherine's luggage still doing here? It's still in the reception…where is she? Is she still here?"

"Which question would you like me to answer first?" Theodora asked calmly.

"Is she here?"

"No!"

"Is that her luggage?"

"Yes!"

"Where is she?"

Nikos started to say something, but Theodora interrupted him.

"We don't know," she said.

"I don't believe you," Jack said defensively.

"Boy, how dare you talk to me like that?"

"Theodora," said Nikos. "*Moro Mou,* calm down. He didn't mean it, and he has the right to know." He then looked at Jack sympathetically. "Sit down, son."

Jack didn't sit down, and he felt so sorry for raising his voice at Theodora who had been like a mother to him, but Theodora couldn't hold a grudge for over a minute. She stood up and gave him a kiss on the cheek and a pat on the back.

"Sit. I'll get you a cup," she said and walked inside.

Once she was inside, Nikos leaned towards him.

"How did the wedding go yesterday?" Nikos asked.

"Flawless. Your little trick worked. How did Maria's parents take it?"

"Yesterday I heard curses that I didn't know even existed," Theodora said interrupting them, placing the cup on the table, and pouring fresh made coffee into it.

"We survived, and they will have to live with it," Nikos said. "What happened has happened."

"Slow down, old man," Theodora said joking. "My Nikos is very philosophical this morning."

Jack smiled despite his distraction and that his brain was concentrating only on one idea: Katherine.

"Katherine came in an hour ago to tell us goodbye,"

Theodora said, reading his mind.

"She left?"

This time Jack learned to ask calmly.

"She did."

"Why didn't she take any of her stuff with her?"

"She said that she didn't need them anymore. She only took a small bag."

Theodora held her hands about fifteen inches apart, indicating the size of a single carry-on bag.

"Did she tell you where is she going?" Jack asked urgently while trying to stay as calm as he could. "I wanted to see her before she left."

"Why?" Nikos interrupted, and for the first time, his tone changed from calm to inquisitive. "So that you can convince her to stay?"

He didn't let Jack respond. Instead he stood up and started lecturing him. Jack hadn't known the old man had that much air in him to speak so much and so firmly and intently. He didn't give Jack a chance to respond before he finished what he had to say.

"You want her to stay so that you would tell her stories of the past? Do you know that you started talking in the past tense, just like me and Theodora? You talk in the past tense as if you are 80 years old. Instead of saying 'I will do', you say 'I did'. Every single day you do the same thing. You wake up, go for a run, go to your room and write, afternoon you play Tavli with me… and … and you know what? Every day I stand in the middle of this courtyard and call your name, and in my heart, I wish that you wouldn't come down, that you are gone, that you have left this place, this island, and went on a new adventure. Jack, I love you like I love my son, and it pains me so much to see you wrapped in the past and not even want to get out of it. Here came the one person who will get you out of your past, and yet you want to pull her in and make her stay. No, I won't allow that."

"From now on, you are not welcome to stay here. This is your last day in this place. As for Katherine, if you really love her and want her, let her stay as far away as possible from this island."

Silence prevailed after Nikos said his last words. Jack sat looking at him, not knowing what to say. His heart sank deeper and deeper in sadness, and his eyes were almost ready to burst into tears.

"You think that if Katherine leaves, you will never see her again," Theodora said, as if she just had a revelation.

What Jack felt all along in his heart was just exposed to the world in a few simple words. He was fixated in the past, when Emily left and didn't come back. That's why he stayed. He had been still waiting for her, but now he wasn't thinking about her anymore. He wasn't waiting for her anymore. He was thinking about Katherine, the woman who released him from his past. The woman that made him believe that Emily was gone for good and would never come back. The woman that made him realize that his life was worth living beyond the boundaries of this island. Santorini wasn't the island, he was.

"I have to go," Jack said as he quickly stood up. "I love you both." He gave each one a kiss on the cheek and turned around and ran towards the main entrance.

Jack stopped and looked back once. He looked up at the window of his room then at the stunned faces of Theodora and Nikos and down upon the stunning view of the caldera for the final time.

"*Andio,*" he called and ran away.

Nikos and Theodora stayed silent for a couple of minutes.

"If we knew that would happen, we would have spoken up a long time ago," Theodora said.

"I guess I have to look for a new *Tavli* partner."

***

"I can give you my bathing suit if you want, or anything else," Maria offered. "It will be a few hours before we reach Mykonos."

"I'm fine. Don't worry about me. I'm tanned enough, and I kinda like this blue dress. Makes me look one with the sea," she said as she stood at the bow.

"Here we go," Yiorgos shouted from the helm.

The boat, coincidentally named *Hera*, after the Greek goddess of marriage, started to move slowly away from the dock. Yiorgos kept the sails down until they cleared the caldera. Hera was around 45 feet long and was a little bit more than 30 years old but looked as if it came off the showroom floor just yesterday, painted in brilliant white.

Maria was wearing a white bikini and was now sitting next to Katherine, leaning into her, whispering to her as they both laughed. Every now and then, they both turned and glanced at Yiorgos and laughed again. Yiorgos felt embarrassed as he knew that his intimate moments with his bride were now being divulged.

They were a couple of hundred feet into the water when Maria stopped talking and listened carefully.

"Can you hear that?" she asked, straining to listen.

"Hear what? I don't hear anything."

"It sounds like someone shouting."

"Maybe these are the echoes of the sounds you both made yesterday," Katherine said and laughed.

"No, no! It was someone calling your name," Maria said. "The only name that Yiorgos screamed on this boat was mine."

They all turned to scan the shoreline and saw a man running at the water's edge.

"Is that Jack?" Yiorgos asked, easing a little on the throttle. "He just jumped into the water!"

The girls ran to the stern and saw a man splashing in the water, now swimming towards them. The man was a good swimmer, but he was struggling because he still had his clothes on. Once he stopped for a second and lifted his hand up and shouted Katherine's name, they were sure that it was Jack.

"He's gonna drown!" Yiorgos shouted in a panic. "I saw him only take his shoes and jacket off. His clothes will drown him! I'm heading back!"

"No! Wait!" Katherine cried. "There's no time!"

Katherine started to take off her dress.

"Jack! Keep your legs moving! I'm coming!"

In her panic, she couldn't reach the zipper, so Maria unzipped it for her. Then she realized that she wasn't wearing a bra. She glanced at Yiorgos, who immediately understood and looked the other way. She took off her dress and was left in her lace panties. She took one last glance at where Jack was and dove into the water.

Jack was still struggling. He used to be a great swimmer, but many years without practice and then getting into the water in his clothes on were holding him back. Adding to that, half way through, he had a cramp in his right leg. The pain was unbearable and caused him to panic. He was in distress both physically and emotionally by the feeling that he was about to lose Katherine again and possibly his own life.

He flailed his arms as he saw Katherine coming towards him, but at that moment, he started going under. He couldn't hold himself up since his legs stopped moving. He panicked more, gasping for air but instead inhaling the sea water, and soon his head slipped below the surface of the water.

Katherine fought to reach him amidst Yiorgos's shouting and Maria's hysterical screams. He started drifting down through the water. As he struggled to come back up, the house key fell from his pocket and down to the sea bed. He tried to dive to retrieve it, but he was too disoriented. At the same moment, Katherine's hand slipped around him and below his arm pit and dragged him back to the surface.

Katherine realized that Jack was unconscious, and she needed to take him to shore, but just as she turned to swim towards the port, she heard Maria shouting her name, and a life preserver splashed next to her. She grabbed it and put it around Jack, and they were both reeled in by Maria. Yiorgos killed the throttle and came to help. They lifted Jack's unresponsive body in first and laid him on his back then Katherine came up.

"Stay back," she ordered as Maria leaned helplessly over Jack. "I got this."

Katherine froze for a second, suddenly overwhelmed by the reality of what was happening, and laid her hand on Jack's cold cheek. Time stopped as she looked down at his handsome features, the man she adored and had almost let go. Then she snapped out of it and immediately started CPR. After the tenth chest compression, Jack's head jerked forward, and he spit out a gush of water and drew in a deep breath. Katherine immediately stopped the compressions and tried to roll him to his side to expel any more sea water, but Jack resisted and lay on his back coughing and still gasping for air.

"A mermaid," he murmured as soon as he opened his eyes and saw Katherine hunching over him topless.

"Mermaids are blond," she said, smiling as tears spilled down her cheeks and onto his face.

Yiorgos held Maria tightly, relieved that Jack was alright. He guided her towards the stern, leaving Katherine and Jack alone at the bow.

"You're foolish and reckless and…" Katherine started to say, but Jack suddenly pulled himself up and stopped her with a kiss.

"I wanted to follow you," he said after their lips unlocked.

"You want me to come back?"

"No, I want to go with you...because you know, today I realized how much I love you."

Katherine knew how much he loved her without him saying it. He loved her enough to almost drown for her. He loved her enough to let go of his past and come after her. He loved her so much that he was willing to leave his self-inflicted exile and follow her. He loved her that much, and she knew it. Her heart was bursting in her chest from her exertion and from being filled with so much love for this man.

"I love you from Santorini to San Francisco," he said breathlessly. Before the last syllable came out of his mouth, his lips were sealed by Katherine's kiss.

About The Author

Alex M Smith was born in 1974 and started writing at an early age, experimenting with poetry and short stories at first. In college, he wrote a romantic short story that was deemed -too hot to publish- in any college publication at that time. Upon his graduation, his father was diagnosed with Lou Gehrig's disease. That changed Alex's plans and brought him down to earth and away from writing. Fifteen years into his career as a self-made entrepreneur, he decided to go back to his first love, writing. In 2012, he published his first novel, The End of Summer, and never looked back.

Printed in Great Britain
by Amazon